"I—I wa...

T.J. choked on his lemonade. "Say again?"

Emily swallowed hard and squared her shoulders. "I said I want you to be my husband."

T.J. blinked. If she'd announced a meteor was hurtling toward earth and was about to land at his feet, he couldn't have been more surprised. Either he was a victim of sunstroke or a stranger had asked him to be her husband!

"You've got the wrong man. You'll have to find someone else to give you a wedding ring."

"Wait! I only intended to ask you to *pretend* to be my husband. And only for one day."

"The answer is no, not for five minutes, let alone one day." Red-blooded man that he was, T.J. might have given Emily Holmes his attention, all right, but she wasn't going to have him for a husband, no matter how tempting she looked in that wisp of a dress she was wearing....

Dear Reader,

This month, Harlequin American Romance delivers your favorite authors and irresistible stories of heart, home and happiness that will surely leave you smiling.

TEXAS SHEIKHS, Harlequin American Romance's scintillating continuity series about a Texas family with royal Arabian blood, continues with *His Shotgun Proposal* by Karen Toller Whittenburg. When Abbie Jones surprised Mac Coleman with the news of her pregnancy, honor demanded he give her his name. But could he give his shotgun bride his heart?

Another wonderful TOTS FOR TEXANS romance from bestselling author Judy Christenberry is in store for you this month with *Struck by the Texas Matchmakers*, in which two children in need of a home and several meddling ladies play matchmakers for a handsome doctor and a beautiful lawyer. Harlequin American Romance's theme promotion, THE WAY WE MET...AND MARRIED, about marriage-of-convenience romances, begins this month with *Bachelor-Auction Bridegroom* by Mollie Molay. And old passions heat up in Leandra Logan's *Family: The Secret Ingredient* when Grace North's first crush, now a single father, returns to town with his precocious little girl and ends up staying under the heroine's roof.

Enjoy this month's offerings and come back next month for more stories guaranteed to touch your heart!

Wishing you happy reading,

Melissa Jeglinski
Associate Senior Editor
Harlequin American Romance

BACHELOR-AUCTION BRIDEGROOM

Mollie Molay

HARLEQUIN®

TORONTO • NEW YORK • LONDON
AMSTERDAM • PARIS • SYDNEY • HAMBURG
STOCKHOLM • ATHENS • TOKYO • MILAN • MADRID
PRAGUE • WARSAW • BUDAPEST • AUCKLAND

"For Jennifer Walsh,
thank you.
Here's to a great future!"

ISBN 0-373-16879-9

BACHELOR-AUCTION BRIDEGROOM

ABOUT THE AUTHOR

After working for a number of years as a logistics contract administrator in the aircraft industry, Mollie Molay turned to a career she found far more satisfying—writing romance novels. Mollie lives in Northridge, California, surrounded by her two daughters and eight grandchildren, many of whom find their way into her books. She enjoys hearing from her readers and welcomes comments. You can write to her at Harlequin Books, 300 East 42nd St., 6th Floor, New York, NY 10017.

Books by Mollie Molay

HARLEQUIN AMERICAN ROMANCE

560—FROM DRIFTER TO DADDY
597—HER TWO HUSBANDS
616—MARRIAGE BY MISTAKE
638—LIKE FATHER, LIKE SON
682—NANNY & THE BODYGUARD
703—OVERNIGHT WIFE
729—WANTED: DADDY
776—FATHER IN TRAINING
779—DADDY BY CHRISTMAS
815—MARRIED BY MIDNIGHT
839—THE GROOM CAME C.O.D.
879—BACHELOR-AUCTION BRIDEGROOM

Don't miss any of our special offers. Write to us at the following address for information on our newest releases.

Harlequin Reader Service
U.S.: 3010 Walden Ave., P.O. Box 1325, Buffalo, NY 14269
Canadian: P.O. Box 609, Fort Erie, Ont. L2A 5X3

BACHELOR #46

Name:	T. J. Kirkpatrick
Age:	33
Hair:	Blond
Eyes:	Blue
Occupation:	Building restorer. Can also be persuaded to masquerade as a pretend husband for a distressed beauty left in the lurch by his look-alike younger brother. Any job—or wife—he accepts gets his full attention!
Best Qualities:	Muscled shoulders. A willingness to break the rules now and again and to respond to the burgeoning chemistry with his pretend spouse makes him irresistible.
Weaknesses:	Beautiful women…one in particular!

Prologue

The auctioneer called for a minimum bid of one hundred dollars. A timid voice at the front of the room echoed the bid. Emily raised her hand and shouted, "One hundred and twenty-five!"

"He's mine," a voice at the back of the room yelled enthusiastically. "Two hundred!"

Emily bit her lower lip and clutched her purse. Her funds were severely limited, and she was rapidly reaching the bottom of her wallet. But time was running out, and she had to have the man. "Two hundred and twenty-five!"

"Let's get real here," called her bidding rival. "The guy's mine. I bid three hundred!" The man on the stage grinned, stuffed his hands in his pockets and winked at Emily.

Emily blinked at the blatant invitation from Number 46. Her first reaction was to brush him off and wait for the next man. After all, she reminded herself, what she had in mind was a business arrangement, not a seduction.

Her second and involuntary reaction surprised her. "Three hundred and fifty!"

The man on the stage raised his eyebrows. A smile of approval curved at the corner of his lips. The crowd began to murmur and crane their necks to look at the latest bidder. Emily wanted to hide.

The auctioneer intoned, "Going, going," and silence filled the room. With the word "gone!" and a crack of a wooden gavel, Number 46, all six feet of him, was hers. The crowd broke into applause. Instead of being elated at her victory, Emily's heart sank to her toes. Now what?

Chapter One

Number 46 watched the winning bidder slowly make her way to the stage to claim him. She appeared to be a conservatively dressed businesswoman with auburn hair, porcelain skin, and hazel eyes the color of an early morning western sunrise. She might be trying to look all business, but her short skirt and slender, shapely legs gave her away.

Something told him that under her carefully groomed exterior was a sensuous woman. In any case, as far as he could see, she was a dream walking. His spirits perked up. Maybe being "rented" as a date for a day wouldn't be so bad after all.

He began to have second thoughts as she drew closer. There was something about her determined expression that telegraphed she was the type that played for keeps. The words "for keeps" weren't even in his vocabulary, and he didn't plan on adding them. Filled with belated misgivings at having volunteered for a bachelor auction, he fervently hoped his escort duties would be brief.

Receipt in hand, his buyer reached his side and glanced down at the program. "Mr. Kirkpatrick?"

He nodded politely and waited for her to identify herself. She blushed, and to his bemusement, her complexion turned a becoming shade of pink. "I'm Emily Holmes."

"Pleased to meet you, Miss Holmes. T. J. Kirkpatrick at your service," he replied politely. "What did you have in mind for the two of us?"

She blushed again.

He gazed at her quizzically. He may have thought she looked like a dream walking, but something about her body language told him there was more behind her bidding on him than met the eye. "You must have had something in mind when you bid for me. Right?"

Her expression was a study in contradictions. She nodded silently. Something was definitely wrong. It began to dawn on him that maybe being auctioned off to a strange woman hadn't been such a good idea. Not even for a charitable cause.

He looked over her head at the cashier, who was watching them with interest. "Stay here for a minute. I'll be right back."

Her hand reached out to stop him. "Where are you going?"

The note of alarm in her voice and her grip on

his arm stopped him in his tracks. "To get your money back for you. It looks to me as if you've changed your mind."

"I haven't. It's not what you think," she protested when his eyes narrowed. "Could we go somewhere private and talk?"

Private. Tim digested the idea for a minute. All of his instincts warned him he was teetering on the edge of deep waters. It was time to set the record straight. "I believe you may have made a mistake, Miss Holmes. Regardless of what this setup looks like, I'm not a professional gigolo."

"I'm not looking for one," she said firmly, squaring her jaw. Sparks of anger filled her eyes. "I won you as an escort for a day fair and square, Mr. Kirkpatrick, and I intend to have you face up to your agreement."

His honor tested, Tim considered falling back on the alternate plan he used whenever his back was against the wall. What had started out as a joke had just lost its humor. A free spirit, the last thing he cared for was to be "won" by anyone, let alone by a woman high on looks and, if she took the auction that seriously, obviously one card short of a full deck.

But first things first. In case he had read the lady wrong, he intended to do the honorable thing. He reached for his wallet. "Here," he said, offering her a wad of bills. "Keep your receipt. I don't know what you had in mind, but *I'll* give you your money back myself. That way you can have an income tax deduction and your money, too.''

''No, thank you,'' she protested, backing away from his outstretched hand. ''I don't want your money. I want you. This receipt tells me you belong to me!''

His thoughts spinning, Tim gazed at his new owner. ''Belong'' sounded too permanent for his peace of mind. He'd have to see to it that their date was brief and took place where they would have lots of company. After all, how much of a problem could one date be as long as he kept it public? He nodded reluctantly.

Emily considered her prize. He was perhaps six feet tall, had brown hair streaked with gold and blue eyes that spoke of California summer skies. To add to her growing misgivings about her choice, he was decidedly too handsome for his own good.

Fortunately, he seemed to have a sense of humor, or he wouldn't have offered himself to the highest bidder. Maybe he thought the whole idea of being on an auction block was a hoot. She didn't.

He wasn't her type, she thought as she gazed into his wary blue eyes. But nevertheless he appeared to be just the man she needed. He had to have a kind heart, or he couldn't have allowed himself to be auctioned off for charity. She tried to ignore the uneasy feeling rushing over her. She was uncertain about her choice, but for better or worse, she was going to go with her instincts and hope for the best. Surely, the man must have a better side to him somewhere.

"Belong to you? In what way?" her prize asked cautiously.

"I want you to come with me and have our picture taken."

He breathed a sigh of relief. "If all you want is a photograph, I guess I can do that." He straightened his tie, ran his fingers through his hair and grinned. "If you ask me, $350 for a photo seems a little high. But if it's a souvenir you want, why not? I'm game."

Emily didn't have the courage to tell him why she wanted to have her picture taken with him. Not yet, and not before she had her photograph. "Good. There's an instant photo shop in the lobby. If you're ready, let's go."

She was pleased to see him take a deep breath and shove his hands into his pockets. "I guess I'm as ready as I'll ever be."

With her prize beside her, Emily took quarters out of her coin purse, poised her head carefully next to his and looked up into his eyes with a bright smile. When she was satisfied they looked like a happily married couple, she dropped in four quarters and pressed the button that gave her a husband. "There!" she said when the photographs slid out of the machine. "Just what I needed."

"That's swell! By the way, thank you for your donation, Miss Holmes," her partner said amiably as he backed out of the booth. "The foundation thanks you, too." Before she could stop him, he waved goodbye and started out of the photo shop.

"Wait a minute!" she called after him. "I forgot to tell you I may need you again tomorrow."

He swung around and stared at her. His wary expression came back. "Tomorrow? You mean the photograph wasn't enough for you?"

She shook her head. A guarded expression came over her face "Maybe. Maybe not."

He smothered a groan. His high hopes for a quick getaway dashed, Tim's heart sank. What she wanted with him was anyone's guess, but it looked as if she intended to get her $350 dollars worth. "Why not get whatever you have in mind over with today?"

"Tomorrow," she repeated firmly. She couldn't tell him she needed one more day to go to plan number two if plan number one failed. Instead, she looked around to make sure no one could overhear her and went on to borrow the street language she'd often heard on television. "A deal is a deal. That is, if you can give a day's work for two days' pay."

He winced as if her challenge hit too close to home. "Of course I can, but to tell the truth, I'm beginning to feel like a lamb being led to slaughter."

"A lamb?" Her eyebrows rose as she considered

the man who looked more like a rogue than a lamb.
"Hardly, Mr. Kirkpatrick. You're the furthest thing
from a lamb I can think of. That's why I wanted
you." She paused long enough for him to get the
message. "And by the way, under the circumstances, you can call me Emily."

"Circumstances?" Instead of looking chastened,
he eyed her suspiciously. "What circumstances
would that be?"

"I'll tell you tomorrow." She reached into her
purse for a roll of the peppermints she chewed on
whenever she was nervous and offered one to him.

"No, thanks," he answered, his mind busy working on how to swim out of muddy waters before he
got in over his head. He wondered just how soon he
could fall back on his tried-and-true backup plan to
get out of the way of trouble. "Why tomorrow and
not today?"

"Tomorrow," she repeated firmly, and popped a
peppermint into her mouth.

His mind was made up. Emily Holmes was not
the woman for him, but he knew just whom she *was*
for. As far as he was concerned, his meeting with
Emily Holmes had been ordained. Just the thought
made him feel virtuous. "Maybe I ought to give you
my business card and an address where you can find
me if you need me. Say around noon?"

She took the card and carefully put it in her purse.
"I'll be there."

PROMPTLY AT TWELVE, Emily showed up at the address noted on the business card T.J. had given her yesterday. She checked the address against the sign in front of the building site and relaxed. T. J. Kirkpatrick, Historical Building Restoration, was a real business. Recalling the calculating look in the man's eyes yesterday, she'd been half-afraid the card had been a fake.

Ahead of her, four men in dusty jeans and worn T-shirts were busy rebuilding a crumbling red brick wall. A weathered sign across the front of the aging structure dated 1939 proclaimed the building to once have been a fire station. Today it looked more like a private building of some sort badly in need of repair. A dozen more men dressed in jeans, sleeveless T-shirts and helmets roamed over the site. When one man removed his hard hat and wiped his forehead, her gaze unerringly found the man she was looking for. All six feet of him.

She was in the right place.

He was wearing leather boots, worn jeans and a shirt open to his slim waist. Rolled-up sleeves revealed muscular forearms. His brow was beaded with sweat. The faint, dark shadow of a beard covered his tanned face. Clearly in charge of the operation, he was muttering to himself as he dried off his face and turned to check the efforts of the work crew.

Yesterday at the auction, she'd decided he wasn't

her type. Today her eyes widened, and her body warmed at the sight of him.

She'd taken their photograph to the law office yesterday afternoon as proof she was married. To her dismay, she'd been told she had to come up with the man himself.

There was something different about the man today, she thought as she waited for him to notice her. He looked a little older, taller, a bit more muscular and, if possible, more attractive. With his sun-tanned skin and muscular chest showing under his open shirt, he didn't look to be quite the same man. In the photograph he'd reluctantly taken with her yesterday, he'd been dressed in a tailored suit, white shirt and paisley tie. An immaculate fop.

As a result, she'd spent a sleepless night planning this meeting and its intended outcome. Now that she was here, she was beginning to have her doubts. What she had in mind, coupled with his sexy appearance, made her wonder if she hadn't gone overboard in her efforts to get his full cooperation. There was a problem. He was still the kind of man a woman liked to dream about, but not the kind of man a woman necessarily takes home with her. After being jilted by her too-handsome-for-his-own-good fiancé, she wasn't going to go down that path again.

The more she gazed at her target, the more uneasy she became. Yesterday, he'd merely been a means for her to get her inheritance. Today, judging from her physical reaction, he'd turned into a flesh-and-blood man, decidedly striking.

His masculine appearance couldn't be ignored, she thought. Not when his every move touched off an answering response in her.

She had to be honest and objective. It was her own appearance that was beginning to worry her. Deliberately calculated to draw T. J. Kirkpatrick's interest and keep it until the task she had in mind for him was safely accomplished, she was afraid she might have overdone her appearance. She sighed and reached for a peppermint.

She might be a librarian whose worldview largely came from books, but she could recognize sensuous attraction when she felt it. And she felt it now. Maybe she would have been better off winning a harmless, ordinary man she wouldn't have needed to impress. Considering the circumstances, sometimes a woman had to do what she had to do to get her man.

The men scattered over the site stopped to stare when she finally caught their attention. Whistles and catcalls filled the air. One or two waved, another threw down a pail and shovel and started toward her. The look in his eyes was clearly predatory. She fought the urge to leave.

T.J. turned to check out the activity. A studied smile pasted on her lips, a woman stood there looking as if she were poised to run. She was dressed in a wisp of a light-blue summer outfit that covered vital areas and little else. Her silky auburn hair flowed around her bare shoulders, and a single gold chain hung around her neck. A green jade charm dangled from the chain and lay between her breasts. When he could tear his gaze away from the jade charm, he noticed she held a small white cardboard box in her hand.

He took a second, calculating look around and decided he'd better check out the visitor before he had a mini-riot on his hands. He waved off the workmen and sauntered toward his visitor.

"May I help you?" His gaze took in the enticing areas of pink-tinged skin at her neck and shoulders, graceful, slender, bare arms and a body carved to perfection. Pink, manicured toes peeked from white sandals that matched her handbag. To his mind, she was the perfect package of femininity.

The way she affected him made his senses whirl and, in spite of his common sense, his body stir. Speculation as to why she was here in the first place blew his mind. He had to remind himself tempting women like her had no place on a job site. Not that he was a monk when it came to admiring and dating beautiful women, but at the moment he had more important things to think about.

"I told you I'd be here today," she answered, following his gaze down her dress. She gave a little shrug in an effort to make the neckline of the dress move up a little higher, with no discernible results. When she noticed his growing interest, she shrugged again. To her chagrin, it only made matters worse. She tried a smile. "I figured this dress was more appropriate for this warm weather than what I was wearing yesterday."

Appropriate? Yesterday?

T.J. glanced over his shoulder at the crew, who were making no bones about their enthusiasm for his unexpected visitor. "Take thirty!" he called before he turned back to his visitor. Behind him, his crew continued to laugh and joke about their visitor. Sure enough, "take thirty" didn't mean a damn when there was a beautiful woman to look at.

He couldn't blame them. He was taken by her, too. The brilliant sun overhead shone on fiery auburn hair and cast a golden glow over her very visible porcelain skin. To add to her appeal, when he got close to her, he discovered that her scent was fresh and minty. Pungent enough to sharpen his senses and add to his growing awareness of her charms.

It took a moment or two before his gaze swung to her intriguing hazel eyes. They were filled with questions. So was he.

Why was an attractive, obviously well-bred woman wandering around the construction site? And why was she dressed in an outfit surely calculated to draw male attention?

"Appropriate for what?" he prompted. When she stared wordlessly at him, he went on patiently. There was no use pushing her, and by now, he was in no mood to try. "How about starting with your name, or is it too much to ask?"

"My name is Emily Holmes. I told you that yesterday," Emily answered, tearing her gaze away from the cleft in his chin. "As for what I have in mind, that's what I came here to tell you. Just as I promised yesterday." She glanced over at their audience and took a deep breath. "Is there someplace where we could talk privately while you have lunch?"

He glanced at his watch, shrugged and smiled. Heck, it was lunchtime anyway—or close to it. "I usually wait for a food truck to show up. Either you're early or they're late. At any rate, I didn't brown-bag it today."

She thrust the white cardboard box at him. "I didn't want you to miss your lunch hour so I had the hotel kitchen put together a box lunch for you."

"Thank you. A free lunch is something no hungry man would pass up." He wiped his hands on a large bandanna he took from his pocket, glanced around the building site and finally pointed to a small grassy area shaded by a single tree. "Hang on while I find something for us to sit on. I wouldn't want you to soil that outfit.'' He cast a lingering glance at her cleavage before he strode away.

Emily bit back her reply and waited while he found, dusted off, and set up two empty crates under the tree. She might be a little underdressed, but at least she had his attention.

A lunch truck sounded its horn and drew up alongside the construction site. The crew cheered and headed for the truck.

''Lemonade?''

''Yes, thank you.'' She took a seat and watched while T.J. ambled over to the truck and ordered two bottles of lemonade and a cup filled with ice. She'd never met a man quite like him. The sun glinted off his warm brown hair. His stride was confident. Yesterday at the auction, he'd appeared to be attracted to her. She hadn't been interested, but today, for some reason, the feeling had become mutual. Not even her ex-fiancé had affected her this way. She shivered at the thought.

T.J. bantered with the truck driver and crew until he had them all laughing. Embarrassed at her own reaction, she didn't know which got to her more: the sound of his easy laughter, or the way those tanned muscles rippled on his chest as he swung his hands.

Either way, T. J. Kirkpatrick could probably charm the birds right out of the trees, she mused as she watched him wave goodbye and stride back to where she waited. When he winked at her, she began to have second thoughts.

Somehow T. J. Kirkpatrick didn't look to be the kind of man who would go quietly wherever she led. Maybe it would have been easier if he weren't every woman's walking dream. She'd have to remind him she'd won him fair and square and that this visit was strictly business. And, while she was at it, she'd remind herself he was the right man for the role she had in mind for him. Nothing more. When her need for his time was over, he'd be expendable.

T.J. handed her a cold bottle of lemonade and a plastic cup filled with ice. He opened the box lunch and looked inside. "Great! Two ham-and-cheese sandwiches, coleslaw, carrot and celery sticks, pickles and chocolate cake!" He looked at her for a long moment, then smiled. "Not bad! Not bad at all!"

She wasn't sure he was still talking about the lunch.

To her discomfiture, he took a swallow of lemonade before his gaze raked her from the top of her head to her toes. "Let's see now, Miss Emily Holmes. To begin with, you act as if we've met before. I don't think so. If we had, I'm sure I would have remembered you.

"To add to the mystery, you show up here dressed in a way clearly calculated to rob a man of his common sense. You bring him a lunch designed to soften him up. And, to top it off, you haven't stopped shivering since you got here." He gestured to the tree that cast its shade above them. "Considering it's ninety degrees in the shade, you can't possibly be cold." He stopped to contemplate her in a way that made her blood run swift and hot. "So, Miss Holmes, if that's your real name, you must want something from me awfully bad."

Mesmerized by the sound of his voice and the vein that throbbed at the side of his throat, Emily found herself lost in the magic of his masculine persona. She would have reached for another peppermint to calm her nerves, but she couldn't move. The problem was the cat had gotten her tongue, butterflies were waltzing around her middle, and her mind had gone blank.

Still, the moment she'd planned down to the smallest detail had arrived. From the look in the man's eyes, she'd obviously reached the point of no return. It was now or never.

She nodded helplessly.

He took another deep swallow of lemonade, wiped his lips with the back of his hand and eyed her thoughtfully. "So, Miss Holmes, just what is it you want from me?"

Emily swallowed hard and took a firm grip on her emotions. If the man thought she was out of her mind, so be it. "I—I want you to be my husband."

Chapter Two

T.J. choked on the lemonade. "Say again?"

She swallowed hard and squared her shoulders. "I said I want you to be my husband."

"That's what I thought I heard you say." T.J. repacked the lunch and thrust the box at her. "Here, you can have this back. You've got the wrong man. You'll have to find someone else to give you a wedding ring. I may be hungry, but I'm not for hire. And certainly not with a box lunch."

"Wait a minute!" She shoved the box at his stomach, forcing him to take a step backward to keep his balance. "You have the wrong impression. I wasn't asking for a wedding ring. I only intended to ask you to *pretend* to be my husband. And only for one day."

T.J. blinked. If she'd announced a meteor was hurtling toward Earth and was about to land at his feet, he couldn't have been more surprised. Either he was a victim of sunstroke or Emily Holmes had asked him to be her husband!

No matter how inviting she looked in that wisp of a dress, neither choice was acceptable. Red-blooded man that he was, T.J may have given Emily Holmes his attention all right, but she wasn't going to have him for a husband.

He shrugged and dropped the box lunch onto the crate at his feet. "The answer is no, not for five minutes, let alone one day. And certainly not while I still have the brains I was born with. Do us both a favor and find someone else."

"I can't," she protested. "You cost me three hundred and fifty dollars. I don't have the time or the money to make up another game plan."

"Well, I'm sorry," he said with a look over his shoulder at the men who were watching them, "I'm not interested. I have a ton of work waiting for me, and I've got to get back to it."

"Wait a minute!" She reached out to stop him. "I'm not finished yet!"

"Sorry, I am." He turned to go back to work, but the distressed look on her face stopped him. "Now look here, Miss Holmes, no matter who you think I am, I'm still not your man." To his chagrin, she looked more determined than ever. "If you ask me, it looks as if someone has taken you for a sucker. Who'd you give the money to?"

"To the Foundation for Homeless Children. They

had a bachelor's auction yesterday at the Beaumont Hotel."

At the mention of the foundation, pieces of the puzzle started to fit together. The answer to the case of mistaken identity was unhappily becoming clear. "I've heard of it," he answered cautiously. "But I still don't know what this has to do with me."

"I bid more for you than I'd expected to. The fact is that I won you for a date fair and square. I didn't have a date in mind yesterday, but I do now."

"A date?" The thought of taking Emily Holmes out to dinner blew his mind, but at least it was better than being a husband. "You'll have to make up your mind, Miss Holmes. Just what is it that you want of me?"

"I told you, I want you to be my husband." When he shook his head, she went on. "You promised to do whatever I asked you to do."

Enough was enough. Frustrated, T.J. rolled his eyes. "I'm telling you it wasn't me. I swear I wasn't even at the auction!"

"Yes, you were. You gave me your business card and agreed to meet me here today," she went on stubbornly. "I can prove it!" She searched in her bag and came up with the business card. "There!"

T.J. reached for the card and muttered under his breath. There were no two ways about it, the card was his. Or at least, his company's. "This must be someone's idea of a joke."

His mind awhirl with possibilities, T.J. fingered the card. Surely not his wheelchair-bound adoptive father. The two of them didn't even look alike.

Cold chills ran down his spine when he recalled his brother joking about his participation in the foundation's bachelor auction. The same foundation that had facilitated his and his brother Tim's adoption. T.J. had been asked to participate in the auction himself, but pleading a heavy schedule, he'd made a generous contribution instead.

The answer to the case of mistaken identity was rapidly becoming clear.

What really blew his mind was Tim's parting comment this morning before he left on an unexpected business trip. Laughing like a loon, he'd told T.J. he was sending him a surprise!

A surprise?

Emily Holmes?

He bit his lower lip. His younger brother's fingerprints were all over this scenario. And not for the first time, either. Trading on their remarkably similar appearances was Tim's traditional and not-too-novel way of getting out of the hot water in which he regularly found himself. T.J. was used to putting up with his nonsense, but sending Emily here today as a surprise was going too far. The time for Tim to grow up had passed.

He took a last, long swallow of lemonade, cleared his throat and plunged into muddy, deep waters. "I suppose I owe you an explanation, Miss Holmes. The fact is, T. J. Kirkpatrick is the name of the family business.''

When he had her frowning attention, he took a deep breath and gestured to the sign behind him. ''Since my dad, my brother and I all have the same initials, it seemed more practical to use T. J. Kirkpatrick for our building restoration business. My father's name is Thornton John, mine is Thomas Jefferson, and my brother is Timothy James.''

Emily's eyes grew wide. ''Don't tell me all of you are called T.J.?''

''Not exactly, but close. My brother and I were renamed when we were adopted and my father, Tim and I all wound up with the same initials. My father is largely retired, so I'm called T.J. now. My brother is called Tim. He's an architect. He should have told you so yesterday instead of giving you this card.'' He smiled wryly. ''Sorry for the misunderstanding.''

Her lips tightened, and her eyes lit up. He realized he hadn't made a dent in her belief that he was the guy at the auction. Not that he blamed her. It wasn't the first time people had reacted in disbelief to the similar initials. But never as badly as now.

She took a small photograph out of her purse and thrust it under his nose. ''Men! I was afraid you'd try to weasel your way out of the deal, and I've turned out to be right. As far as I'm concerned, you made up that ridiculous story. It doesn't wash with me, Mr. Kirkpatrick. I have this picture we took together yesterday to prove you and I were together. Everything I've told you is true.''

T.J. smothered a groan and reached for the photograph. It was the type of instant photograph a person could take at a drugstore, an airport or a hotel for twenty-five or fifty cents. He studied it carefully, the truth shimmering before his eyes. There was no doubt about it. The culprit in this caper was Tim.

"I swear this isn't me," he said, raising his right hand. "Hold on a minute and I'll prove it to you." He looked back at the work crew covertly admiring Emily. "My crew will back me up."

"Don't waste your time!" Emily retorted, her eyes blazing fire. "I wouldn't believe any of them if they swore on a stack of Bibles. They're probably afraid they'll be fired if they don't agree with you."

In spite of his frustration, there was something about Emily Holmes that struck a chord in him. He'd never been attracted to passive personalities, women included. Hell, he wasn't one himself. What did attract him to Emily was the way she was willing to fight for what she wanted. It was just too bad *he* was what she wanted.

Tim's reason for sending Emily to the building site as a surprise for him was fast becoming clear. It was a setup by his comedian of a brother calculated to put Emily and him together.

Although he'd made a point of avoiding lasting

relationships, he was no saint. For that matter, he'd had his share of dates and that was as far as he was prepared to go. The last thing he needed or wanted was to have Tim set him up with a woman who was looking for a husband.

"Sorry, there's a strong resemblance between my brother and I, but this isn't me," he said, mentally kicking Tim. "I was here working overtime with a building inspector yesterday afternoon."

He handed the photograph back and started to explain again that he and his brother Tim looked so much alike they were often taken for twins. As he tried to ignore Emily's attraction, he had to convince the lady he didn't intend to be her husband. Not to pretend. Not ever.

Then he gazed into Emily's proud, innocent hazel eyes.

Skimpy attention-getting attire and an innate sensuality aside, T.J. sensed there was a vulnerability about Emily Holmes. He'd been in the business world long enough to know people weren't always what they seemed, and that included Emily. He was even willing to bet she wasn't a sexpot or a flirt out to get her man. What he did sense was that, for some unknown reason, she needed him desperately.

His first instinct had been to turn her down. His second was to reconsider. Maybe there was some way to help her without getting too involved.

He thought of trying to reach his brother. Make

him come back to face up to his "commitment."
Bad idea, he thought with certainty as he gazed into
Emily's troubled eyes. Left to Tim's devil-may-care
clutches, the lady would be in deeper trouble than
ever.

Mulling over his choices, he felt guilty, although
he wasn't sure why. After all, while Tim had been
busy matchmaking, he was the one who had been
taking care of the family business.

If his brains were functioning properly, he'd make
his apologies for his brother and get back to work.
And yet, as he studied the firebrand in front of him,
he had the strong feeling she was clearly in need of
his services.

What was one day out of his life?

And why did she have to look at him with such
proud and trusting eyes?

He motioned to Emily to sit down and tried a
sensible, if not reasonable, approach. "Let's talk this
over, okay?" She nodded, but he had the sinking
feeling she wasn't going to give an inch. "Mind
telling me why you need a husband so desperately,
and why you didn't explain yesterday?"

The glint in her eyes told him he wasn't going to
like her answer. "Because I wasn't sure I would
need you today."

He smothered a sigh. "If you ask me, there's
nothing simple about any of this. As far as I'm concerned, three hundred and fifty dollars has earned

me the right to know the entire scenario. Besides,'' he added with a wry smile, ''I figure I'm entitled to make sure the masquerade would be on the up-and-up.''

When she bit her lip, he had the sinking feeling that whatever plan she was about to share with him wasn't going to be strictly legitimate. ''Anything we can get arrested for?'' he went on to ask. ''I'd hate to wind up in jail.''

''Of course not! What do you take me for?''

She tried to look insulted, but he sensed a hint of uncertainty in her voice. ''You tell me, Miss Holmes. If I'm going to be your husband, however briefly—'' he rushed to make clear ''—I need to know the whole story.''

She hesitated and eyed him with suspicion. ''Does that mean you've decided to go along with me?''

He could tell by her frown she wasn't too happy with him. ''Maybe,'' he said reluctantly. ''It all depends on the facts. Just give them to me straight.''

For fear the truth would scare him off, Emily debated the wisdom of sharing the whole story with T.J. What she wanted him to do wasn't exactly honest, but surely it couldn't get them arrested. She mentally crossed her fingers and plunged right in. Lies, even white lies, didn't come easily to her.

''My great-aunt Emily passed away recently and left me some property in Venice,'' she began. ''I'm her only relative. I was named after her.''

To her relief, T.J. began to look interested. His blue eyes focused on her. "Venice, Italy?"

"No, Venice, California. It's a small suburb outside of Los Angeles."

"Yeah, I know the place," he agreed. "The story of the area has always fascinated me. I remember hearing that seventy years ago a builder tried to re-create the original Venice, canals and all. Poor guy went broke when the Great Depression hit."

"That's the place," Emily agreed. "My aunt told me he built the canals and a house or two and ran out of money when the depression hit. She and my late uncle bought one of them for a song." The wistful smile that curved her lips touched him in spite of his determination to stay clear of women like her, no matter how desirable. "I used to visit during the summers when I was a little girl and dream I was in Italy."

Gazing into Emily's smile, T.J. began to imagine her as a little girl dreaming of faraway places. Such thoughts were not only dangerous, he told himself, they were too like the "husband" scenario she proposed. The next thing he'd be doing was picturing a little girl of his own. A little girl with auburn hair and hazel eyes just like her mother's.

"Interesting," he said, eyeing Emily in a speculative way that made her senses spin and her cheeks warm up. "But what does that have to do with me pretending to be your husband?"

Emily took a deep breath and decided to go the whole nine yards. "Aunt Emily used to keep after me to settle down and start a family." When T.J. raised an eyebrow, she felt herself blush. "I know it sounds a bit old-fashioned, but after my broken engagement, Aunt Emily obviously worried I would be left alone the way she was after her husband passed away. I suppose that was why she left me the property with the provision I had to have a husband of my own in order to inherit."

Mental wheels started to turn. For the first time, a ray of hope sprang into T.J.'s mind. "Pardon me for asking, but couldn't you solve your problem by asking your former fiancé to do you a favor and pose as your husband?"

"No way," she replied. A hard look came into her eyes. "Not when he left me for another woman. Under the circumstances, I don't want him to know about the inheritance."

With that door closed, T.J. thought rapidly. "The more I think about it, I can't believe the marriage clause in your aunt's will is legal. Or that a probate court would hold you to it." He studied the hazel eyes that revealed so much of her thoughts. "You don't really believe it, either, do you?"

"I'm not sure," she answered. "The lawyer's letter looked legitimate. I figured it would be best to line up a man before I did anything else. It seemed to be the easiest and quickest way to solve the problem.''

"What about the photograph you showed me? Couldn't you show it to the lawyer as proof that you're a married woman?''

She shook her head. "I tried doing that this morning before I got here, but the lawyer wouldn't buy it. He wants to meet my husband. And, now that he's seen the photograph, I can't ask anyone else to come with me. It has to be you.''

T.J. glanced at the empty lemonade bottle and wished it had been something stronger. "It's a gamble, you know. The guy might be smarter than you think.''

"Maybe, but I figured I'd cover all my bases.'' The corners of Emily's proud eyes glinted with tears. "I'm sorry. But I'm already in so deep, I don't think I have a choice. My husband has to be you.''

T.J. gave up. A promise made by his brother to a woman like Emily Holmes was a promise he somehow felt obligated to keep. She obviously was innocent and deserved better. He'd have to take one day at a time. "When do we start?''

To his dismay, a look of hope came over her face. "This afternoon, four o'clock at my aunt's lawyer's office.''

He stopped to consider his commitment. Was he biting off more than he could chew? "And how long do we have to keep up the masquerade?''

"As long as it takes to convince the man you're my husband." She paused and looked worried. "Just don't forget to act as though we were recently married."

T.J. digested her reply. He came up with an answer that, under different circumstances might have actually been inviting if it had been his idea. Newlyweds? A pretend marriage, with hugs and kisses? With a woman as beautiful and fascinating as Emily Holmes?

Under the present circumstances, the sound of the scenario began to trouble him.

Scenes of his early childhood flashed through his mind. Terrifying scenes of himself and his little brother, both too young to understand their father had abandoned them. Or to understand why their mother had decided she couldn't cope alone and had taken him and his brother to the Foundation for Homeless Children before she left.

A product of a failed marriage, abandonment and a series of foster homes, he'd vowed he would remain single until he found the right woman. And then only after he could be certain their marriage would provide a decent and loving home for their children. A marriage that would last.

Certainly not a pretend marriage that would merely last for an afternoon. And all for a piece of real estate?

He gazed solemnly at the anxiety in Emily's eyes

as she waited for his answer. And the slight tight-ening in her lips, no matter how she tried to hide it. He couldn't help but be moved. Maybe owning the piece of real estate was as important to her as his dreams of a perfect marriage and family were to him.

"Just what does this property consist of that you're so set on acquiring?"

"An old wooden cottage," she answered with a hopeful smile. "The last time I saw it the paint was peeling, there was a hole in the roof, and the lawn had become weeds and dandelions. It wasn't any-thing like the cottage where I used to spend my sum-mers as a little girl. It broke my heart. I suppose that's one reason why I decided to sell after I in-herit."

"And the other reason?"

"The job that's waiting for me up north."

When the sparkle in Emily's eyes dimmed, T.J.'s heart ached for her. No one's dream should end with a dilapidated wooden cottage. If Emily had been his real wife, he would have restored it for her.

Restoring vintage buildings was more than a pro-fession to him. He loved to recreate the hopes and dreams that had gone into their creation.

"I remember hiding behind the curtains of a win-dow seat overlooking the canal and dreaming of see-ing the real Venice someday," she went on, the wistful smile back on her face. "And that's what I intend to do now—see the real Venice."

As she spoke, T.J. pictured a young Emily hiding behind curtains, dreaming innocent childhood dreams. He felt compassion for the child obviously still in her. And, for that matter, the child within him.

He had his own dreams, too. Dreams he couldn't pursue. He had responsibilities to his invalid father, his brother, and the foundation that had brought them all together. Marriage and a family of his own had taken a back seat.

The irony of it all was he was about to pretend to be married to a woman he hadn't set eyes on until an hour ago.

Gazing into Emily's eyes, there was no longer any doubt he was doing the right thing in filling in for his brother. For a day. Further than that, he wasn't prepared to go.

"Hey, boss," a loud voice shouted. "What's next, or are we through for the day?"

Startled out of his reverie, T.J. turned back. Clouds of dust covered the work site where a truck was delivering additional used bricks. Someone had turned on a CD player and strains of music filled the air. Several of the work men had disappeared from view. At this rate, it would be touch-and-go for the restoration project to come in on time. He'd been so engrossed in Emily's story, he hadn't noticed how much time had passed.

Wait until he got his hands on his brother!

What troubled him was that he'd always been an either/or type of guy, with no gray in between. "The truth and nothing but the truth" had always been his motto. Yet here he was, trading his convictions for the look in a pair of innocent hazel eyes.

He felt like a fraud for letting Emily believe he was Tim. Thinking of what might happen to Emily if he didn't go along with her, he couldn't help himself. "I'll put the men back to work and see you back at the hotel. By the way, you don't happen to have the address of the Venice property on you, do you?"

She rummaged in her purse and handed him a slip of paper. "I was hoping you'd ask. See you around three-thirty? You won't forget, will you?"

As soon as Emily was out of earshot, T.J. called to his foreman. "Take over for me this afternoon, Duke. I've got an important appointment."

Duke pointedly glanced over T.J.'s shoulder. "With the babe?"

"With the lady!" T.J. corrected him sharply. His gut instinct told him Emily Holmes was every inch a lady, no matter how she was dressed. Or what kind of outlandish ideas she came up with.

Troubled, T.J. watched Emily disappear around

the corner. The hope in her voice and the appeal in her unforgettable eyes stirred unwelcome emotions in him. Emotions he had no time for. He had to remember this was a game and only a game.

Chapter Three

It took T.J. twenty minutes to reach the address in Venice. And twenty seconds to realize Emily had inherited a treasure. A gem, a jewel of Depression architecture and surely of historical value.

To add to the ambience of the setting, salty air blew in from of the Pacific Ocean, no more than a block away. Newly reworked canals ran in front of the property and new condominiums filled the once-empty lots.

A restorer of vintage buildings, T.J. recognized a one-of-a-kind survivor of the Depression era in the cottage on the property Emily had described. Built of wood, genuine lathe and plaster with beveled glass windows, the weathered white cottage fronted the canal where bridges crossed over to the other side. A new condominium complex filled the lot next door.

The land on which the cottage sat was surely worth a small fortune, he mused as he paced the walk in front of the cottage. Gazing at the weathered frame dwelling and picturing the interior treasures that must surely be inside, his mind rebelled at the thought the cottage would be razed once Emily sold it.

There had to be an alternative. He could offer to buy the cottage in order to save it. Before he did, should he tell her up front how valuable he thought the property was? Was thinking of buying it from her even ethical?

For that matter, was it ethical to masquerade as Emily's husband and go along with her fantasy for insuring her inheritance?

Thought after troubled thought tumbled through T.J.'s mind. He respected Emily's desire to live out her dream, but at one time, the cottage had been someone's dream, too. There had to be some way to satisfy Emily and save the cottage at the same time.

He sighed, glanced at his watch and went to his car. He still had to clean up and meet Emily at the hotel. Without time to make plans or to investigate the lawyer's honesty, he had to go along with Emily for now. But he had bigger ideas if her plan failed.

He called her from the hotel's front desk. While he was waiting, he strolled over to check out ''The World of Posters,'' a sampling of the early motion picture movie posters to be auctioned off by Sotheby's. He studied the *Adventures of Robin Hood* poster, circa 1938. Price: $12,000 to $18,000. A 1940 *Pinocchio* poster priced at $5,000 to $8,000. A*Wizard of Oz* poster offered at a starting bid of $9,000 to $12,000.

A discreet notice mentioned the rare posters would be put up for sale at Sotheby's auction gallery next week.

He'd spent hours in old movie houses researching early architecture and interiors for authenticity in his restoration business. His interest had soon turned into a genuine respect for the dreams of yesterday, of which the posters were prime examples. What he was admiring was, in his mind at least, priceless.

"Beautiful, aren't they?" Emily's wistful voice sounded behind him. "I'd love to be able to buy the *Wizard of Oz* poster. Maybe because of Dorothy's Auntie Em. She reminded me of my own Aunt Emily."

"I was more sympathetic to the Straw Man wishing he had a brain," T.J. laughed. "When I was a kid, I used to think I was missing a brain, too. Especially when my grades weren't as good as Dad thought they ought to be."

Emily smiled. "Maybe I'll be able to buy a poster like this after I sell my inheritance."

"Let me buy the property from you," T.J. offered impulsively. "You can get started making some of your dreams come true."

She looked up in surprise. "That's considerate of

you, but I'm afraid the cottage is very old. It can't be worth much."

"It is to me," T.J. said, attempting to visualize the interior of the cottage. "I'm in the building restoration business, remember? Finding a building like that cottage is like finding a treasure." When she looked surprised, he added, "I drove by to take a look at it on my way over here."

"Then you know what condition it's in. It would take a lot of money to fix it up. Maybe it should come down."

Telling Emily about his suspicion the property was more valuable than she realized might be premature, he thought uneasily. His conscience prodded him to at least tell her part of the truth. "Maybe you'll want to have the cottage restored yourself. I'll be happy to help."

"Thank you, no. I'm not going to live there," she replied. "Selling the property is the only way I can turn some of my childhood dreams into reality."

"Speaking of reality," he said soberly, "maybe we ought to check out the marriage clause in your aunt's will before we see the lawyer? I'm not sure, but I can't believe it's legal."

"You may be right." Emily led the way out of the hotel lobby into the crowded street. "But I'm in so deep with the lawyer now, I'll have to go through with the marriage bit first."

T.J.'s convictions warred with his desire to help

her. He and his brother might look alike, but he was older by five years. Surely the difference showed in a photograph. ''I think I ought to tell you I don't think the lawyer will believe I'm the man in the photograph.''

''Don't even think about it!'' Emily stopped short and turned around to confront him.

Caught by surprise, T.J. plowed into Emily and rocked her on her feet. Instinctively, his arms went around her to help her regain her balance.

To his satisfaction, she felt soft where a woman should be soft, and she smelled like summer flowers. Her auburn hair smelled of scented soap and an essence of peppermint clung to her. Her lips parted in a gasp of surprise.

He couldn't help himself. Before he could stop to think, he instinctively bent to take those lips with his. Instead of pushing away, she unexpectedly closed her eyes, put her arms around his neck and leaned into his kiss.

That was the signal T.J. was waiting for. He pressed her lips apart and sought a haven for his tongue in her minty-scented mouth. When she responded with a soft moan, he probed gently, questioningly. In response, her tongue dueled with his.

His knees felt weak. Time stood still. His resolve to keep his distance from Emily began to fade. He forgot he was her temporary husband and that she was just passing through his life. He told himself he was just giving in to an impulse. An impulse that had been born the moment his startled gaze had connected with her warm hazel eyes.

Emily responded to T.J.'s kisses with a mind at war with her body. She was no stranger to kisses, after all, she'd been engaged. But this kiss, this man, were different from the embraces she's shared with her ex-fiancé.

Where Sean's kisses had been demanding, this man's kiss was warm and tender and invited her response. Where Sean's embraces had been quick and self-serving, this man's embrace invited her to linger. When his hands ran over her back and pressed her close to him, she forgot her ex-fiancé and the errand that had brought her here.

Until the doorman coughed.

Startled, she saw they were surrounded by amused spectators. A few clapped. A passing motorist sounded his horn.

Emily tried to pull away. How could she have been so stupid? After Sean had jilted her for another woman, she'd sworn off becoming involved with a man, any man, hadn't she? And yet here she was trading kisses with a man she'd met only yesterday. And wouldn't see again after today.

"T.J., we have to stop," she whispered into his lips. "We're making a spectacle out of ourselves."

The doorman coughed again. This time he got T.J.'s attention.

What was he doing kissing Emily like this anyway? T.J. wondered as he opened his arms and let Emily go. She was a stranger, after all. An unknown quantity. A woman he would never have met if it hadn't been for Tim and his crazy matchmaking ideas.

"What did you think you were doing?" Emily sputtered. "We don't even know each other!"

"I guess I was practicing," he answered for want of a sensible explanation. How could he explain his unexplainable desire to take her in his arms the moment he laid eyes on her? "You did mention hugs and kisses."

"Not in public and not in broad daylight, for heaven's sake!" She looked appalled and cuter than ever.

Better than in private and in the dark, T.J. thought as he regarded well-kissed rosy lips and sparkling hazel eyes that revealed so much. Given the right setting, he knew damn well he wouldn't have been able to stop with mere hugs and kisses. Not when Emily had been an eager partner.

Emily averted her eyes and forced her heart to return to a normal beat. She'd told him of her dream of visiting Italy, but she hadn't spoken of another dream she'd nurtured until Sean had jilted her. A dream of home, hearth, and a lifetime of happiness with a man she loved, and who loved her. A man like T.J.?

She should have known better than to respond to his kiss, no matter how wonderful he made her feel. Yesterday at the auction she'd sensed he was a rogue at heart and maybe a little dangerous. True or not, she didn't intend to become another conquest of his or of any other man's.

She pasted on a tight smile so that anyone watching her would think she enjoyed T.J.'s embrace. "I meant I wanted you to be lovable at the lawyer's office. Not out here on the street!"

He grinned. "Sorry about that. I'm a strong believer that practice makes perfect. We've got to make it look good, don't we?"

Emily straightened her suit collar, tucked stray tendrils of hair behind her ears. But not before she reached into her purse for a roll of peppermints. "We'll have to hurry, or we'll be late."

By now, T.J. was ready for anything that would take his mind off Emily's lips. He held out his hand for a peppermint and popped it in his mouth. "Come on, my car is parked around the corner."

"No need," Emily answered as she started off down the street. "The lawyer's office is just two blocks away. That's why I chose this hotel."

"Gotcha," T.J. murmured gratefully. The pungent peppermint wasn't doing much to keep his mind off Emily's lips or the satisfying way she'd felt in his arm. Failing a cold shower, a brisk walk might do the trick.

The concrete buildings and the sounds of traffic along their way proved to be a distraction. By the time they reached their destination, T.J. had cooled off. Some, but not all the way. He was as aware of Emily as ever. And, judging from the overt glances she kept sending his way, the feeling was mutual.

Wilbur Daniels, the lawyer behind the gilt letters on the door to his office, regarded Emily quietly when his secretary announced them. As soon as they were seated, she introduced T.J. as her husband. Daniels raised an eyebrow. "Interesting. May I see the photograph again?"

"Of course." With a warning glance at T.J., Emily handed over the small photograph, then reached into her purse for another peppermint.

By now T.J. recognized that the pungent candy was a sure sign Emily was nervous. And that beneath her outward bravado, there had to be a growing fear her plans could blow up and take her inheritance with it.

Between Tim's well-intentioned matchmaking and the way he'd just manhandled Emily on a public street, T.J. felt he owed her. He had to give her a chance at the inheritance she had coming. Even if it took him posing as her husband. But first, there was the matter of the disturbing marriage clause.

He put his arm around Emily's shoulders, hugged her to him and planted what he hoped was a welcoming kiss on her lips. He felt her soft moan of protest but was grateful she didn't pull away. "Atta girl," he whispered into her lips.

Daniels glanced from T.J. to the small picture and back again. "Kind of blurry, don't you think?"

"It's not studio quality, if that's what you mean." T.J. mustered a proud grin. "The truth is, when I met Emily I fell head over heels in love with her." He laughed and squeezed Emily again. "I didn't give her time to change her mind, let alone to have wedding pictures taken. I couldn't wait to..." His voice trailed off. The wink he gave the lawyer finished the sentence.

"T.J.!" Emily admonished. A blush covered her face. "Mr. Daniels will think—"

T.J. broke in and finished the sentence for her. "He'll think we're a happily married couple, sweetheart."

Daniels frowned. "Frankly, Mr. Kirkpatrick, in itself, the photograph is hardly proof of your marriage." He tossed the picture on his desk, sat back in his leather chair and steepled his hands. "I'm afraid I'll have to see your marriage certificate."

"For Pete's sakes! I didn't think I had to carry it with me," T.J. replied with a frown. "Did you, Em?"

Em. Emily stared at her temporary husband. How could he know that Em was the loving nickname her aunt had used for her? What was there about T.J.

that made her heart beat faster even while her temper boiled?

"Of course not! No one carries around their marriage certificate." Emily pulled away from T.J.'s arm and leaned across the mahogany desk. "Mr. Daniels. It's my belief you're making this more difficult for me than you need to!"

Daniels stood and closed the folder on his desk. "Not at all, Miss Holmes. It's a matter of following my client's wishes. And the law governing probate."

"Mrs. Kirkpatrick! And don't you forget it!" T.J. exploded. He jumped to his feet before he realized that if he didn't watch himself, he'd be knee-deep in a possibly illegal conspiracy.

"Mrs. Kirkpatrick," the lawyer amended. His complexion blanched, but he held his ground. "It doesn't matter what I think. As an officer of the court, it is my duty to make sure your aunt's wishes are carried out. And the wishes contained in her last will and testament clearly state you must be married in order to inherit her estate."

T.J. sensed Daniels was far from convinced he and Emily were married. He sent her a warning glance. Whatever it would take to insure she got her inheritance wasn't going to be accomplished here, or today.

Daniels glanced at Emily. "I'm going out of town

for a few days. That should give you time to produce the certificate.''

As far as T.J. was concerned, the man's trip out of town was too convenient to be true. Without coming right out and saying he doubted Emily was a married woman, Daniels was giving Emily time to hang herself.

T.J. intended to make sure Emily understood she was headed for trouble if she insisted they were married in order to gain her inheritance. Without a license or a marriage certificate, there had to be another way.

Back on the street, T.J. drew Emily into a small coffee shop. The comforting odor of freshly brewed coffee and the scent of warm cinnamon sticky buns were tantalizing. But they didn't do much to ease the growing premonition sending icicles running up and down his spine.

He motioned to a table and headed for the serving counter.

''I hope you're not thinking of doing something irrational or illegal,'' he said when he rejoined Emily. ''If you are, count me out.'' He set the paper cups of hot coffee on the table and glanced at her clenched hands and tense lips.

She nodded her thanks. ''Of course I'm not.''

''You're not?'' He wasn't convinced, not when she couldn't meet his eyes.

''I'm not,'' she repeated. ''I'm not even sure

where to go from here. But I can tell you this. I'm not going to give up. My aunt wanted me to have the property, and I intend to fight for it.''

"I'm sure she did," T.J. soothed. "It's just too bad she added the marriage clause to her will. Maybe you ought to consult a lawyer of your own?"

"A lawyer might help," Emily agreed. "Unfortunately, I don't know any lawyers around here. I'd have to go back home to Placerville to find one."

T.J. held his tongue. He was afraid if he gave her his own lawyer's telephone number, he would be getting more involved with Emily than was wise. He was already too attracted to her for his own good.

Emily silently drank her coffee and mulled over her options. With none in sight, going back home and talking things over with her mother was the logical thing to do.

There was a problem: with T.J. across the table, she was in no mood to think logically. Not after the way she'd reacted to his unexpected embrace. Not after the way she'd reacted to his kisses, either. And certainly not when her senses were in a turmoil.

After she'd been jilted by Sean Foster, she'd sworn off men, hadn't she?

She still had her dream of visiting Italy, didn't she?

So why was she even thinking of the amazing way she'd felt after T.J. had taken her in his arms and kissed her senseless? Or why she could hardly wait for him to do it again?

"I think I'll go back to the hotel and try to take a nap," she finally remarked. Her head throbbed and her stomach was in knots. "These have been very trying days."

"Sure," T.J. answered, wishing he could take a nap with her. Maybe it was just as well he hadn't been invited. He couldn't have stopped with a nap. He settled for getting to his feet and reaching for her hand. "Come on, I'll walk you back to the hotel."

Emily's comment about trying days was the understatement of the year. Courtesy of his brother, T.J. had gone from being a bachelor to being a married man in a matter of hours. Married to a woman he didn't know.

He'd participated in a masquerade that looked as if it didn't have a prayer of succeeding. The way things were now, he'd be lucky if he didn't wind up getting charged with intent to commit fraud.

If that weren't enough to keep his mind and body in turmoil, he was becoming more and more attracted to Emily Holmes.

He glanced uneasily at the woman who, intentionally or not, was rapidly turning his safe and ordered world around into a place where he couldn't recognize himself. He was even afraid to imagine what her next move in this wacky scenario would be. Her ideas, at least so far, had been naive and maybe harmless. Unless he was mistaken, the next idea would probably be illegal.

Instead of thinking of taking a nap with Emily, he should have taken his head out to be examined.

"Trying days" was putting it mildly, Emily mused as she and T.J. walked back to the hotel. T.J.'s continued silence didn't help, either.

Either he'd forgotten their earlier embrace, or he'd already dismissed their brief encounter. Maybe she'd given him too much credit for being sincere. Maybe she was just another conquest of his, after all.

T.J.'s devil-may-care attitude at the bachelor auction yesterday should have warned her he wasn't reliable.

Meeting him this morning again at the construction site and having to coerce him into honoring his promise should have been proof of his character.

To top off a confusing day, winding up in his arms in front of the hotel this afternoon and returning his embrace as though they were lovers had been the most unsettling event of all.

She glanced at a more dangerous-than-ever T.J. out of the corner of her eye. How could she have been so foolish to have asked him to masquerade as her husband?

Chapter Four

Back to setting bricks in mortar, T.J.'s thoughts continued to linger on the troubled look in Emily's eyes.

What the hell was wrong with him? One minute he was saying goodbye to Emily, and the next, he was kicking himself for not sticking around to help her.

He'd done his best to live up to the bargain Tim had left him, hadn't he? Even when his personal convictions had been against posing as his brother.

A visit to the lawyer with Emily had been one thing, faking a marriage certificate was another.

Further than the visit, he told himself firmly, he wasn't prepared to go.

The next scheme the lady had up her sleeve had to be a fake marriage certificate. The thought of that request coming down the pike had been enough for him to throw in the towel and say goodbye.

Sure, she hadn't gotten around to asking him to help her with the fake marriage certificate, but as sure as his name was Thomas Jefferson Kirkpatrick, that had been in the works.

So why did he feel as if he'd betrayed the trust Emily had placed in him?

And why did Emily's air of desperation and the glint of tears in her captivating eyes continue to haunt him?

The pile of used bricks in front of him began to shimmer in front of his eyes. To add to his misery, the blazing sun beating down on his back was making him his head swim in spite of the hard hat he wore. And if that wasn't enough to try a man's soul, his stomach was at odds with his breakfast. He didn't know why. He ate four slices of bacon, two eggs and toast every morning with no side effects. Today, as the morning wore on, he was feeling worse than ever.

He reached for the bottle of water and took a long swallow to clear his head. When his vision began to blur, he poured water into his hand and drew it across his forehead. His head still pounded. To add to his problems, he had an uneasy feeling he had left something important undone.

"Emily," he muttered to himself. Whatever was wrong with him, it had to have something to do with Emily. Through a growing haze, the sound of her name was enough to almost make him smile. It wasn't only their kiss he remembered, although he was honest enough to admit it was a big part of her attraction.

The devious way her mind worked fascinated him. The way her eyes gave away her inner thoughts just before she popped another peppermint into her mouth was another. To add to her attraction, there had been the satisfying moments when he'd held her in his arms.

He muttered his frustration and laid another brick. He might be fresh out of common sense, but there was no way around the problem. Pure and simple and straight to the point, he missed Emily.

In saner moments he would have known better.

Duke strolled up. "So, how did the date with the babe, er, the lady, go last night, boss?"

"It wasn't a date." T.J. wiped the beads of sweat from his forehead and headed for the shade of the oak tree while he was still able to navigate.

Bad choice.

The tree only served to remind him of the bargain he'd made with Emily: he would pose as Tim long enough for her to get her inheritance. Hooked by the grateful look in Emily's expressive hazel eyes, the mission had seemed so simple—a visit to her lawyer and then a goodbye.

The problem was that he hadn't reckoned on Emily's magnetic attraction. Or her lingering minty scent and the memory of their spontaneous embrace.

Somewhere along the way he must have lost his mind.

Duke tagged along after him. "Not a date? Hey man, that's not the way it looked. You couldn't take your eyes off the lady. Can't say I blame you. I wouldn't mind dating her myself. Is she available?"

T.J. swung around, the drum in his head beating louder than ever, his stomach about to rebel. "If that's all you have on your mind, get lost!"

"Hold your fire," Duke protested. "I came to tell you your dad called while you were off yesterday afternoon doing whatever it was you say you weren't doing."

T.J. scowled. In his present weakened condition, the last thing he needed was sexual innuendo. "Any message?"

"Nope," Duke answered cheerfully. "The boss said he'd see you today."

T.J. eyed his foreman. He wore a wide grin and looked too pleased with himself to be innocent. "What else did you tell him?"

Duke shrugged. "I could have mentioned the ba—the lady and the sexy outfit she was wearing."

"Jeez!" T.J. cussed under his breath. "That's all I need the way I feel. Testosterone talk. Go back to work."

When Duke left whistling cheerfully, T.J. dropped down on the wooden crate and took a deep breath. It hadn't taken Duke's remarks to make him realize that what was bothering him wasn't so much the

heat as some unfinished business. He'd been taught
from day one never to leave for tomorrow what he
should do today. No wonder he felt uneasy.

His mind's eye flashed back to Emily. How she'd
gazed at him as if he, and only he, could be her
knight in shining armor. Instead of saving her, he'd
chickened out at the earliest opportunity. What kind
of a hero did that make him?

Maybe that was why he felt so lousy.

Duke was right. In her slip of a sundress, Emily
had been a bundle of femininity fetching enough to
draw the attention of every man within eyesight.

She'd certainly been all woman. To his chagrin,
his instinctive response to her had been all male. Her
sensuality and his reaction must have come through
loud and clear or Duke wouldn't have commented
on it. At his age, he should have known better than
to let sex appeal get to him.

How Emily felt about him was another story, he
mused unhappily, but a promise made was no promise kept when there was unfinished business to take
care of.

All the more reason for him to go back to the
hotel, stop Emily from coming up with a fake marriage certificate and think of another idea. If she
wound up in trouble, he'd never be able to live with
himself.

The point was, he chided himself, he knew
enough about the transfer of real estate holdings to
be aware that printing up a fake marriage certificate

had to be illegal. Emily might be willing to take a chance, but not him. He had his conscience, the family business and the Kirkpatrick name to consider. The last thing he wanted to do was get into trouble with the law.

A horn sounded a tattoo, and T.J. glanced up to see his father's specially equipped van roll up to the work site. Since the automobile accident two years ago, he'd conducted business from home.

T.J. took another swallow of tepid water and sauntered to meet the van. "What brings you here this morning, Dad?"

"Just dropped in to say hello," his father replied. "Give me a minute."

With a push of a button, the motorized front seat sank to earth level. With the push of another button, the side door slid open to reveal a wheelchair.

T.J. knew his father needed to feel self-sufficient, so he waited until his father was seated in the chair.

"So, what's up, Dad?"

His father wheeled himself under the tree and locked the chair's brakes. "What makes you think something's up?"

T.J. regarded his father through a growing haze. He loved his father, owed him big. "I know you, Dad. You wouldn't have come here instead of phoning if you didn't have something on your mind."

Instead of looking him in the eye, his father fussed with the lock on the wheelchair. "Just checking out your progress on the station, for one."

T.J. shook his head and tried to clear it long enough to think. "No problem, we've been working overtime so we're right on schedule. Finished gutting most of the interior two days ago. Right now, we're rebuilding two of the walls."

"You've left the fireman's pole intact, I hope," his father reminded him. "The Swansons want to build an iron circular staircase around the pole to give the place some atmosphere."

"Or maybe they want to play fireman." T.J. gazed at the building and tried to visualize the old fire station as someone's home. "Good thing there are some people who are interested in restoring old buildings instead of tearing them down."

His father raised a questioning eyebrow. "What brought that on?"

T.J. glanced over to where Duke was making a show of being busy. "Tell you what, Dad. You spill your story, and I'll spill mine."

His father laughed. "Yeah, well, it's not something I wanted to discuss over the telephone. I've lined up a new job. How would you like to move to Hawaii for a year?"

A year in paradise? Who wouldn't? T.J. knew his spirits should be flying; instead his heart sank like a lead balloon. Leave Emily to fight for her inheritance alone? Let someone take advantage of her? He couldn't, not with a clear conscience. Who would help her and keep her out of trouble if he didn't?

"I don't think so," he said, trying to focus on his

father's offer. "At least, not now. I've got something on the back burner to take care of."

"A lady?"

T.J. recognized Duke's fingerprints all over the question. "Not entirely." He wiped his throbbing brow. It would be a miracle if he didn't pass out in his father's lap. "On the other hand, maybe, but not for long."

"Heck." His father laughed. "You're beginning to sound like your brother. What do you mean, not for long?"

T.J. mustered a weak grin. When it came to Emily, he was beginning to feel like Tim. Except that he normally wasn't the love-'em-and-leave-'em kind of guy. When he found the right woman, he'd play for keeps.

He told his father about Emily, her mistaking him for Tim, and his decision to cover for Tim. He ended with the visit to her aunt's lawyer to collect her inheritance.

"Doesn't sound like you," his father said as he eyed T.J. "You're as straight as an arrow. The lady must have had some power of persuasion to get you to go along with a wild scheme like that. So tell me, is it Emily you're interested in, or is it the Venice property?"

"Emily, I guess," T.J. answered. "But to be honest, I'd like to save the cottage from a wrecking ball. It's the best example of Depression architecture I've ever seen. The location in front of a real canal makes it one of a kind.''

''Well, no harm done as far as I can see,'' his father said cheerfully. ''Even though Tim was the one to involve you, you did the right thing. But,'' his father added with a faint smile, ''I get the feeling the story isn't over. Or am I wrong?''

''No,'' T.J. confessed. ''I don't know if it's too much exposure to the sun that has me feeling so confused, but you're right. Fact is, I can't seem to put Emily out of my mind.''

''Shows you're just as human as the rest of us, my boy. If the lady is as wonderful as you say she is, you're lucky.'' His father eyed him shrewdly. ''To tell the truth, son, I'd almost given up on you providing me with a couple of grandchildren.''

''Grandchildren? No way. I was talking about helping Emily, not marrying her.'' T.J. frowned at the idea. ''Hell, I'm only thirty-three. There's plenty of time for grandchildren. At the rate Tim falls in and out of love, he'll bite the dust and beat me to fatherhood. I know better. I have too many responsibilities to think about a wife and children.''

''Maybe so, but don't forget I'm not getting any younger. So, as for this Emily of yours, go ahead and try to help her. Just try not to get arrested. There's the family reputation to think of.''

T.J. felt too weak to laugh. His widowed father was in his early sixties and handsome enough for women to take a second look—wheelchair and all.

As far as romancing Emily, hell, he wasn't that far gone. He'd know the right woman when he found her, and he hadn't found her yet.

Helping Emily was another story. He'd already made up his mind to go to the hotel and offer his advice. In spite of the strong attraction he felt for her, advice was where he intended to draw the line.

All the talk about grandchildren made him shiver. His father might dismiss T.J.'s responsibilities, but not him. He owed his adoptive father big, and he was man enough to remember it.

"How about the Hawaii deal?" his father asked when they were back at the van.

"I don't think so, Dad. Why don't you ask Tim to go out there and size up the project? At the rate he's going, he needs something to keep him out of trouble."

"Good idea. I'll think about it," his father called out the window before he drove away.

At four o'clock, T.J. headed for home. A quick, cold shower and a cup of hot, black coffee didn't make him feel any better. What he needed was a shot of brandy and a good night's sleep, but he couldn't take the time. He had to find Emily before she did something stupid.

He climbed into his car, turned on the air conditioner and headed for the Beaumont Hotel. Maybe he should have called first, but he had the uneasy feeling if he stopped moving, he'd fall flat on his face.

"Is Miss Emily Holmes in?"

The desk clerk checked his computer and nodded. "Shall I announce you, sir?"

"The name's Kirkpatrick," T.J. managed to answer. "Go ahead, but please make it quick." When the desk clerk raised a questioning eyebrow, T.J. held on to the counter. "Sorry," he said, "but the way the floor keeps moving makes me feel like hell. I've got to sit down pretty soon, or I'm going to fall down."

The clerk glanced around him warily. "Moving, sir?"

"Yeah," T.J. said as he grasped the counter more firmly. "I sure hate these aftershocks, don't you? I keep waiting for the big one."

"Aftershocks?" The clerk looked apprehensive. "I didn't feel any earth movement."

T.J. shrugged. "Well, I did. Maybe you'd better call Miss Holmes now."

"Yes, sir." The clerk kept a wary eye on T.J. while he made the call. "Yes, ma'am. I'll send Mr. Kirkpatrick right up." He regarded T.J. doubtfully for a moment before he gave in. "Room 1224, Mr. Kirkpatrick. Miss Holmes is waiting for you."

T.J. took the elevator to the twelfth floor and carefully made his way down the hall. Ahead of him, a door opened and Emily appeared. She was wearing a robe, her hair was caught up on top of her head, and her feet were bare. It looked as if she was about to take a shower. He barely made it to her side before he staggered.

Emily rushed to steady him. "You look terrible! What happened? What are you doing here?"

"One question at a time, please," he replied. "But before I answer, do you mind if we go inside where I can sit down?"

Emily helped him inside her room and to an upholstered armchair. His face was white, his eyes were glazed, and his forehead was studded with beads of sweat. A vein at the side of his throat throbbed as if he'd been running. His open shirt revealed moisture on his chest. In his present condition, she was surprised he'd been able to stand on his feet.

No wonder the desk clerk had called back and warned her her visitor looked and acted strange. He'd been right. And what was this about aftershocks?

"Are you sure you feel well enough to be here tonight?" she asked. "It looks as if you would have been better off home in bed."

"I'll feel better as soon as the walls and the floor stop moving." She could tell T.J. was trying hard to keep his eyes open.

She felt his forehead. In spite of the air-conditioning, his head was burning up. "You feel very warm," she said. "Are you sure you're okay?"

T.J. nodded. "Maybe it was too much sun, the water, or maybe something I ate this morning," he muttered, "but I have to admit I feel rotten." He shuddered and held his hand over his eyes. "Those damn aftershocks don't help."

Aftershocks? With an answer like that, Emily knew T.J. had to be sicker than he thought. She had heard enough about the effects of too much exposure to the sun to begin to worry. She felt his head again, headed for the telephone and asked to speak to a doctor.

"The doctor is too busy to come up right now," she told T.J. when she hung up. "But he's given me some instructions on what to do until he gets here."

T.J. mumbled something, leaned his head against the chair and seemed to fall asleep.

She tried to remember the doctor's instructions. Bed rest, if she could get him into bed, sounded doable. But salt tablets? Have the patient drink as much liquid as he could hold? Rub him with cold towels to get his temperature down? It wasn't going to be easy. With T.J. in his present condition, she'd have to do it all on her own. She didn't have a prayer of getting him to cooperate.

She mulled over the option of calling back the doctor and pleading stupidity. The more she debated the thought, she realized it was no option at all. But it *was* payback time.

T.J. had stuck his neck out, gone with her to the lawyer's office when, clearly, he hadn't wanted to. She didn't know why he was here now, but the least she could do was help him when he obviously needed her.

Except that she didn't have any salt tablets and didn't know where she could find any. A cold water rub was possible, but she'd have to take his clothes off. The thought of his nude, masculine body made her own body warm. She eyed him uneasily and steeled herself to do the right thing.

It took a lot of coaxing before she was able to persuade T.J. to stand up and put an arm around her shoulders. With a firm grip on his wrist and her arm around his waist, she slowly led him the few short steps to the double bed. "Here, you can rest while we talk." With a sigh of relief, he let go of her shoulder and fell facedown on the bed. A snore told her he was fast asleep.

Emily bit her lip and considered trying to wake him up. In his present condition, there was no way he was going to move unless she did it for him. She took a firm grip on one of his shoulders, pushed, and shoved until she managed to turn him over on his back. "T.J., wake up," she commanded. "If I'm going to help you, I could use a little cooperation."

It was like speaking to the wall.

His eyes remained closed, his breath was labored and beads of sweat continued to pour from his forehead. He smelled of perspiration and shaving lotion and was out like a light. She felt the side of his neck for his pulse. It was beating madly. To complicate matters, he was obviously too sick to undress himself. She was on her own.

With a sigh, she gently brushed T.J.'s bronze hair from his forehead. Trying to discount her sensual response to him wasn't going to be easy, but she steeled herself to ignore it. After her failed engagement, she wasn't going to let any sexual attraction get in her way. She'd been down that road before.

She debated her choices, then took off his shoes and socks and, accompanied by his groans of protest, wrestled him out of his jacket and damp shirt. She felt herself flush at what would come next. What would T.J. think when he woke up and found himself naked? What would he say once he realized she'd been the one to undress him?

Enough was enough, she thought as she headed for the bathroom with the chrome pitcher she'd found on the nightstand. She'd undress him only as far as his jeans. He'd have to start getting better from the top of his head to his waist. Further than that, she couldn't bring herself to go.

The rest of him would have to take their chances.

As for getting water in him, her chances of that were slim to none.

He lay quietly enough when she started on his forehead. So far, so good. It wasn't until she rubbed the cold towel across his throat and nude shoulders that he moaned and flinched.

"Take it easy, T.J.," she soothed. "Take it easy. This will only last a few minutes. You're going to feel better, soon.'' To her relief, he seemed to relax at the sound of her voice.

She wrung out another wet towel and started on his shoulders. She had reached his muscular chest when he stirred again.

''Emily, is that you?''

''Yes,'' she answered with a reassuring a pat on his shoulder. ''I'm here.''

To her dismay, he reached up and pulled her down beside him. Before she could protest or move, he threw an arm over her waist, a leg over her hips and turned his face into the hollow between her breasts.

Helpless to move, Emily froze. When he slowly moved his hand from her waist to push her robe aside, and tenderly brushed her breasts, she couldn't have moved if she tried. Not even when sparks of sensual electricity followed where his hand led.

What was he going to do next? she wondered uneasily. And what would she do if he went any further? She was tempted to relax. After all, who would know besides her? Before she had a chance to decide, he hugged her to him and fell back against the pillows, fast asleep.

She let out her breath. Considering her response to his unexpected embrace the other day, it was just as well the decision was out of her hands. She shook his shoulder. ''T.J.? You have to let me get up!'' To her dismay, she was rewarded by a satisfied smile and a snore.

She debated whether she should try to move from under his sheltering arm and leg or let him sleep. If she couldn't finish rubbing him down with cold towels, at least he was getting the rest the doctor ordered. Sleep was good for him, wasn't it?

Emily glanced around the small room, just large enough to accommodate the double bed, the upholstered chair and a small table positioned by the window. Moonlight had begun to drift in through the curtains. Her choice was to remain on the double bed with him or, if she was able to move him off her, to spend an uncomfortable night in the chair.

She glanced down at T.J. He was either unconscious or sound asleep. She smothered the temptation to feel his forehead to see if his fever had lifted. Considering her enjoyable reaction to his nude chest against her own almost nude body, touching wasn't a good idea.

It was going to be a long night.

Chapter Five

"Em?"

Emily groaned, cuddled deeper into the bedding and tried to ignore the voice calling her. Since only one person other than her late aunt and her mother called her Em, she had to be dreaming.

"Em!" the voice called again. Her heart softened at the sound of her nickname. She opened her eyes to see a bewildered T.J. propped up on an elbow and gazing down at her in surprise. "What are you doing in my bed?"

Her nostalgic thoughts vanished with a heartbeat.

She sat up, pulled the cover to her chin and gazed up into clouded eyes inches from her own. She remembered thinking she should have tried to put a barrier of pillows between them, but with his limp weight over her, she hadn't had a chance.

She stared into his smoky-blue eyes. How could she tell him why they were in bed together, or explain why she hadn't pulled herself loose sometime during the night? She had a feeling he wouldn't believe her if she did. She had a hard time believing it herself.

She was embarrassed. And not only at the memory of the heat that suffused her after he'd thrown his arm and leg across her and touched her intimately before he'd fallen asleep. It was the way his unconscious embrace and his soft breath against her cheek had felt so right that she'd given in to the inevitable and fallen asleep.

Last night, those thoughts had seemed harmless. She'd planned to work herself loose before morning. She'd figured he'd never know she remained all night. Now that he was awake and staring down at her with puzzled eyes, it was a different story.

"You must have really been out of it when you showed up here last night," she answered, looking at the creases of sleep on his bronzed face, glad that the color was almost normal again. He'd looked so deadly white the night before. "You looked awful, but you look better now."

"Glad to hear it," he mumbled, running a shaking hand across his forehead. She caught herself wanting to touch his forehead with her lips to check his fever.

"Sorry, I'm afraid I don't know where 'here' is," he answered gazing around the room. "And I still don't understand what you're doing in my bed."

Conscious of his eyes on her, Emily inched out

from under him and wrapped her robe more securely around her. "Your bed? You must be sicker than I thought. This is my hotel room and my bed. You've been here all night."

"No way," he answered firmly, and struggled to get up and on his feet. "Give a guy some credit. I never would have forgotten something as intimate as that."

Emily went to the dresser to brush her hair, avoiding his eyes in the mirror. The way she was responding to him, she couldn't trust herself to meet his gaze. She tried to concentrate on his health. If he could try to make a joke out of finding himself in bed with her, he had to be feeling better. Enough was enough.

Now that he was awake, she was through trying to be Florence Nightingale. She turned back into the room. T.J. hadn't moved off the bed, but his calculating gaze was on her.

"Are you trying to tell me you don't remember showing up at my hotel room last night too sick to walk and ready to pass out?"

"No," he answered, rubbing the back of his neck and eyeing the rumpled bed. "If you don't mind. I'd still like to know how we got in bed together."

"I had the choice of letting you lie in the hotel corridor or getting you into bed. You should be thankful I chose the latter." When she saw the growing awareness in T.J.'s eyes, she became more embarrassed than ever. Just what did he think had happened last night?

"So you were the one who put me in here with you?" His eyes roamed over her with a calculating glint.

Emily would have felt more annoyed at the glint if a warmth hadn't started at her middle and begun making its way south. Men! Give them an inch, and they'll take a mile. "I was trying to help you get in bed before you collapsed. I repeat, I didn't plan on getting in there with you."

Weak as he was, T.J. had to smother a grin. He took in the soft curves of her body, which were only partially hidden under her robe, and wondered how he could have forgotten spending the night in bed with her. Her explanation might account for him winding up in her bed, but what really blew his mind was his waking up to find her in his arms. "And then what happened?"

"You grabbed me and pulled me into bed with you. And before you make something out of that, let me assure you that was all!"

T.J. smiled when her complexion turned a delicious pink. She obviously was no more immune to him than he was to her.

What had actually taken place between them during the night was the question. Judging from the wary look in Emily's eyes, it was a question that, as a gentleman, he couldn't bring himself to ask. Not if he didn't want her to throw the hairbrush at him.

He felt embarrassed and, strangely, embarrassed at being embarrassed. He tried to focus, to remember details. Had they made love or hadn't they?

In spite of the throbbing in his head, the thought seemed to please him. Under her wary gaze, the possibility became pure fantasy. If he'd put the fantasy into action with a woman like Emily, how could he not remember?

He cleared his throat. "I think I should tell you the last thing I remember is feeling lousy enough to knock off work early. I even remember thinking of going home to take a shower, but after that, not a blip."

He checked out Emily's robe as he spoke. The possibility dawned on him that she had nothing on under it. "Is there something about last night I ought to remember?" he asked cautiously. "If so, I'll take the blame. I apologize."

"Apologize?" Emily echoed. To his amusement, she looked offended. Because he'd made love to her, or because he hadn't? "Apologize for what? I told you, you were out like a light. From what I could tell, you were in no shape to do much more than breathe."

"Oh, I don't know," he answered, his manhood threatened. "I've never had any complaints."

He reconsidered his attempt to lighten up the situation when Emily stared back at him with a fierce expression. Whatever she was thinking, it wasn't about his performance. More likely, she thought he was out of his mind and wondering which cheek of his to slap.

Maybe it wasn't fair to push her. After all, from what she'd said, she'd practically saved his life. He'd wanted to help her, hadn't he? Maybe he ought to stay on good terms with her. At least, until he could get his act together. "Would it help if I plead temporary insanity?"

"If that's all you have to say, let me tell you I've had enough of this nonsense," Emily replied grimly. "Now that you're awake, just tell me whom to call to come and get you."

T.J. decided he wasn't ready to leave and that he'd better keep the rest of his questions to himself or he'd be out on his throbbing head. His apology obviously hadn't been accepted, and he wasn't home free. She was a very desirable woman, and she had her pride.

Sane or sick as a dog, there was no denying he was powerfully attracted to Emily. But a relationship? No way. Falling in love, let alone considering marriage, would only get in the way of the responsibilities he had to his family. And to the vow he'd made to himself. Emily represented the trouble he'd sworn to avoid: a woman with a mission and itchy feet to boot.

As for himself, he'd found his own mission the day he'd been adopted. His feet were firmly planted on the ground that surrounded the T.J. Kirkpatrick family and family business. At least, they had been before he met Emily.

He glanced at the clock on the nightstand. To his dismay, it was almost dawn and had to be the morning after the night before. A night he appeared to have spent in Emily's bed.

It wasn't like him.

"I've got to get up," he muttered. He sat up, threw his legs over the side of the bed and tried to get on his feet. Sharp shards of pain shot through his head, the room tilted and his stomach rebelled.

Emily rushed to hold him down. "Don't move," she ordered, and tried to push him back to bed. "As long as you're here you might as well stay in bed. The doctor said you needed bed rest for a few days."

T.J. cast a bleary eye at Emily. If he weren't already at death's door, he would have appreciated her tousled auburn hair, her flushed cheeks and her concerned hazel eyes. Eyes that told him that, while she might act annoyed, their attraction was mutual.

Instead of lingering and debating the issue, he shook off her hand and headed unsteadily for the bathroom. A long, cold shower was in order.

Thankfully alone, T.J. tried to remember deciding to find Emily and came up empty. The last thing he

clearly remembered was having a devil of a headache, discussing Emily's situation with his father
and then heading for home. How he'd managed to
wind up at Emily's hotel and in her bed with her in
his arms was anyone's guess.

He threw cold water over his face and stared at
the wan apparition in the mirror. He looked like hell
and didn't feel much better, mentally or physically.

In the mirror, the reflection of Emily's panty hose
and underwear hanging on a thin plastic clothesline
over the tub behind him made him uneasy. For a
man who'd sworn off lasting relationships, the scene
was as domestic as they came.

He glanced down at his chest and, for the first
time, realized it was bare. The cold tiles on the bathroom floor reminded him of his bare feet. Thank
goodness he still had his jeans on.

He held on to the sink, too dizzy to even consider
a cold shower. Considering the shape he was in, how
had he found the strength to spend the night romancing a beautiful woman like Emily?

Maybe he ought to go back and apologize again.

He toweled off his face and, after a lingering look
in the mirror, gingerly made his way back into the
bedroom.

"Emily, I'd like to..." No sooner had he started
his apology than he was interrupted by a knock on
the door. He glanced down at his bare feet and chest,
at Emily's sheer robe and tousled hair and grimaced.

The signs of a romantic interlude were obvious. "Who's that?"

"Wait!" Emily whispered frantically. "Don't answer the door until I have a chance to change. It's probably the doctor. He told me he'd drop by this morning to check on you." She rushed to the closet for her clothes.

"Or the hotel detective," T.J. muttered to himself. He glanced around a room he didn't remember entering and at the tangled sheets on the bed. "Where's my shirt and the rest of my clothes?"

"On the floor," she answered. "I didn't have time to pick them up. Not after you..."

T.J. snapped to attention. "After I what?"

"Never mind," she said over her shoulder as she headed for the bathroom. "Just answer the door."

By the time T.J. shrugged into his shirt, their caller was pounding on the door. When he opened it, a portly man carrying a doctor's bag stood there with his hand raised to knock again. He looked worried.

"I'm Dr. Sanchez," he huffed. "I was about to call hotel security and have them open the door to see if you and the missus were okay."

"The missus? What missus are you talking about?"

"Your wife, of course. She called about you, but she didn't sound so good over the telephone, either. Is she sick, too?" The doctor eyed T.J.'s open, wrinkled shirt, bare feet and rumpled bed. "Sleep in your clothes?"

Shakier than ever, T.J. rocked back on his feet and looked longingly at the bed. "No. I usually sleep in the raw."

"Kind of risky, considering you've had an overdose of sun and the air-conditioning in here," Dr. Sanchez said with a measuring look at T.J. "You might as well sit down while I take your temperature and check your blood pressure."

"I'm fine," T.J. protested. The sooner he could get rid of the doctor, the sooner he could talk to Emily and get back to safer territory.

"Good," the doctor answered. "In that case, I guess you won't mind if I make sure." He motioned to the chair, opened his bag, took out a thermometer and popped it into T.J.'s mouth. "By the way, where's the little lady?"

T.J. motioned to the bathroom door just as Emily rushed out of the bathroom. She was dressed in her memorable sundress, her hair tied back with a ribbon. Nice, T.J. thought through a haze, but she'd looked a hell of a lot more interesting in her silk robe.

"Dr. Sanchez?"

"Dr. Fred Sanchez," he answered amiably. He took the thermometer out of T.J.'s mouth, checked it and nodded. To T.J.'s relief, the blood pressure cuff came next. "I'm sorry I couldn't get here any earlier, Mrs. Holmes. When you didn't call back last night, I figured you and the mister were doing okay with the instructions I gave you over the phone.''

Emily sent a warning look at T.J. when he opened his mouth to answer. ''Thank you, Doctor. I think my husband is feeling a little better,'' she said with an adoring smile at T.J.

''Seems to be,'' the doctor answered. ''His temperature is normal, although his blood pressure is a little high. A few days in bed should do the trick. Keep drinking water. Get some rest and you'll do fine, young man. You too, Mrs. Holmes. By the way,'' he added, his hand on the doorknob, ''if you had told hotel reservations you were newlyweds, I'm sure they would have given you a larger room.'' He winked at Emily. ''Maybe, even the honeymoon suite. Unless the honeymoon is over, give 'em a call. Maybe it's not too late.''

T.J. spoke up the minute the door closed behind the doctor. ''Husband? *Mr. Holmes?* Honeymoon? Who told him I'm your husband?''

''I did. I couldn't let the doctor think you were just spending the night, could I?'' Emily answered adamantly, pulling at the neckline of her dress. ''Letting him think we were honeymooning was embarrassing enough.''

T.J. struggled to get himself together. Pretend husband or not, for a man determined to put marriage on the back burner, he wasn't doing too well at staying single. "Why not? People do it all the time."

"And what makes you think that I do?" she countered. Round one was over, he thought, but she looked ready for round two. "In case you've forgotten, you arrived here on your own. I certainly didn't issue an invitation."

T.J. bit back a retort. She had him fair and square. But, right or wrong, his reasons for appearing at her hotel room didn't change the fact that he hadn't had a peaceful moment from the time Emily had shown up in his life.

It was all his fault. In a moment of weakness, he'd decided to play Sir Lancelot to Emily's Queen Guinevere and gone with her to her lawyer. He even remembered his final goodbye the other day. Now he found himself in her hotel room and too sick to leave.

He should have taken his father up on his offer of a working vacation in Hawaii. At least, there would have been three thousand miles between him and Emily.

Under different circumstances, he might have gone for a woman like Emily. But not at this stage in his life. Something about this whole caper made him feel like a gigolo.

As if things weren't bad enough, Emily was broadcasting news of their "marriage" to anyone who'd listen.

He eyed his nemesis. Even with a headache that gave no evidence of clearing up anytime soon, he was able to reduce his problem to one simple sentence. He and Emily were becoming too close for comfort. He had to return to his orderly life.

Summoning the last of his strength, he decided it was time to get his act together. He looked around for his shoes and jacket. After one step, the room spun around him. He reached for the armchair. It was hold on or fall down.

Emily rushed to throw her arms around him. "Where do you think you're going? You heard the doctor. You belong in bed."

"Em," he said wearily as he shook off her hand and dropped into the armchair, "we have to talk."

"You can talk after you're in bed," she answered. She sized him up and debated the wisdom of trying to get him back in bed by herself. The chair won out. "You're going to have a relapse if you keep this up!"

T.J. wiped beads of sweat from his forehead. The take-charge part of him hated to admit it, but he was too weak to argue. On the other hand, the idea of getting back in bed with Emily funneling water down his throat was unthinkable.

"No way," he answered. "I'm sure my dad will come here to pick me up if I call him. I can go to bed when I get home." He looked at the telephone on the nightstand. The telephone looked to be a mile away. Now that he was beginning to remember he was here to help Emily, maybe he'd call later. "We have to talk about the lawyer."

Emily looked suspicious. He didn't blame her. He didn't blame her for not trusting him. Certainly not after all he'd put her through last night. To make matters worse, he wasn't sure he could trust himself to make sense in his present condition.

"About this marriage bit," he said weakly. "You have to stop telling people we're married. It's not getting you anywhere." At her silence he tried to remember why she'd picked him for a bridegroom. "How did you come up with the fool idea to hire a husband in the first place?"

"I told you the other day, at the charity bachelor auction." Emily poured him a glass of water and handed it to him. "You must be weaker than I thought. As for my idea, there was nothing foolish about it. I needed a man to pretend to be my husband. From the moment you walked on the stage something told me you were the man for me. You looked dangerous."

T.J. felt his manhood redeemed. He straightened up. "How dangerous?" he asked with a lopsided grin.

"Dangerous enough," she replied, eyeing him as if he were a teenager on the make. "You cost me three hundred and fifty dollars, and nothing has come of it. So, drink up, just like the doctor ordered.''

"Ah yes, the charity auction," T.J. echoed as a dim memory of the charity auction and his brother's role in it surfaced. Thank goodness he remembered that much. It was last night's bedroom scenario and the part he'd played in it that he was having a difficult time remembering. "A big mistake. I never thought it would work." He emptied the glass in one long swallow and shuddered. Too bad Emily hadn't realized life was one big joke to Tim.

Emily regarded him silently. "Unfortunately, you turned out to be right," she agreed, and poured him another glass. "I came up with the idea because I thought it was the quickest way to settle my aunt's will." She didn't tell him she'd been influenced by the need to get far away from the man who'd jilted her, as soon as possible.

"Too bad it didn't turn out that way," T.J. muttered, eyeing the second glass of water apprehensively. No way was he going to reach for it. If he drank it, she'd only pour him another. He felt bad enough without becoming waterlogged.

"But you still came back." She eyed him with an expression that hit him where it hurt—right between the eyes.

Now that his reasons for showing up at Emily's hotel room were coming back to him, T.J.'s conscience told him he owed her an honest, direct answer.

He couldn't tell Emily he'd come back yesterday because he hadn't been able to get her out of his mind. That he still remembered how she'd felt in his arms for a few brief, memorable moments that had ended in a kiss he would remember. Or to tell her that her wounded eyes had continued to haunt him each time he'd said goodbye.

He couldn't bring himself to share those thoughts; not without opening a door to possibilities he intended to keep closed.

The marriage scenario was definitely out.

On the other hand, there was no harm in trying to help her. Maybe he'd be able to live with his conscience.

"I remember I came back because I suspected your aunt Emily's lawyer was taking you for a ride. I came back to tell you so, to see if we could put our heads together and straighten him out."

When Emily's eyes lit up, so did T.J.'s spirits.

"I'm glad I'm not the only one to think so," she answered. "I sensed he wasn't honest from the first time I met him."

T.J. was too weak to point out Emily had been as dishonest in her own way as the lawyer had been in his. Or to remind her calling Daniels dishonest was a case of the pot calling the kettle black.

"I'm afraid Daniels didn't have to be a rocket

scientist to suspect something wasn't right when you showed up with a photograph of your husband. You clinched his suspicions when you came back with me. But don't worry, Em. After I get through with him, you'll be on your way in no time.''

The sound of someone vacuuming outside the door covered Emily's answer. Just as well, T.J. thought wearily. All this talk had left him too tired to think, let alone share any more of his thoughts or plans. He'd have to take care of them later. With a sigh, he gave up, leaned his head against the back of the chair and closed his eyes.

Emily grabbed the glass of water before it fell out of T.J.'s hand. She knew from the worn-out look of him that, although his memory seemed to have returned, he was still too sick to move. He needed his rest more than he needed the water. She set the glass on the dresser.

Intending to ask housekeeping to change the linens on the bed, she took a blanket and gently tucked it around him. He muttered ''Em'' in his sleep.

Bemused, she gazed at golden-brown eyelashes resting on suntanned cheeks. At the smile that curved at the corner of his lips. Was she in his dreams?

It was strange that he should have called her Em, a nickname of endearment given to her by her aunt. A name that made her feel cherished, wanted. A nickname her former fiancé had thought too juvenile to use.

She didn't doubt that somewhere in this unexpected adventure, she had begun to care for T.J. Or that, somehow, he'd begun to care for her. She tucked in a corner of the blanket that had fallen away from his bare chest and smothered a sigh of regret.

She also knew he intended to say goodbye after he helped her settle her inheritance. Maybe this time it would be forever.

There was no future for them. No more than there had been a future with Sean when he'd found a wealthy widow. Her former fiancé hadn't wanted her. It was clear that T.J. didn't want her, either.

No matter, she told herself. T.J. didn't owe her anything, not after today. He'd come back to warn her, maybe even to help her, out of the goodness of his heart.

She'd nurse him until he recovered. She would gratefully accept what help he might still intend to offer. After she settled with the lawyer, she'd sell her inheritance and live out the dream of visiting the real Venice, a dream she'd cherished from the time she had been a young girl.

Alone.

Chapter Six

T.J. stirred and opened his eyes. To his relief, his headache was gone, his mind was clear and his vision sharp. He still felt a little shaky, but he'd learned a lesson the hard way. Stay out of the sun.

He'd been in the building business from the time he'd learned how to wield a hammer. He certainly should have known better than to continue to work under the blazing sun, especially after he began to see double. The result of his stupid behavior was to get himself sidelined into Emily's bed, a place he ordinarily wouldn't have minded being found, except for the fact he was here to help Emily. Not to romance her.

He glanced around him. A blanket had been tucked around his waist, and a glass of water waited on the dresser—both clear signs Emily had been taking care of him instead of him taking care of her. Judging from the scenes he was beginning to remember, he owed her big.

Normally a take-charge guy, T.J. felt like a dog about abandoning Emily after their visit to Daniels, instead of finding a way to help her. Now that his mind was clearer, there was no way he was going to leave her to the sharks.

Things were going to change.

He stood, paused long enough to make certain he wasn't going to fall over and slowly made his way to the bed where Emily was sleeping. With her tousled auburn hair spread across the pristine pillow, her creamy flesh rosy with sleep, Emily looked as vulnerable and as innocent as a child. No wonder Daniels thought he could take advantage of her, he mused as he willed himself to remember he was here to help Emily with her inheritance. Romance had to take a back seat.

T.J. sensed Emily was stronger than he'd given her credit for. Although, he thought with a wry grin, the zany way she'd gone about gaining her inheritance was unusual and somehow fitting.

Waiting for her to awaken, it occurred to him that he knew little about her outside of her foray into the auction. Why would her aunt insist Emily be a married woman when remaining single wasn't a crime? And why wouldn't Emily, a thoroughly modern woman, have contested the will?

Clearly, outside of her brief foray into an engagement, remaining single had been Emily's choice. Gazing down at the sleeping Emily, she sure didn't look as though she would have had to buy a pretend bridegroom. Not when she was intelligent and beautiful and could have had a real husband by now.

He paced the room in his rumpled jeans, looking for the rest of his clothing. Someone had neatly set his shoes at the foot of the bed, and had even taken time to tuck his socks inside. His jacket hung from a wooden rack. Everything looked neater than he felt. A shower was obviously in order.

Inside the bathroom, Emily's panty hose and underwear were gone. Fresh terry-cloth bathrobes were hanging on the door and fresh towels gleamed from a heated rack. A disposable razor and toothbrush waited on the sink. A check of the medicine cabinet revealed a bottle of mouthwash and shaving lotion.

Muttering his relief, T.J. shucked his shirt, shaved with one eye on the door, undressed and headed for a long, hot shower. He thought of Emily and the way his attraction continued to cloud his vow to keep her at arm's length. The problem was, although he'd made up his mind to help her and to put her out of his life, he couldn't put her out of his mind. He had to remember that no matter how she lit his fire, any thought of romancing Emily would have to go on the back burner.

Dressed again, he was buttoning his shirt when he heard Emily mutter in her sleep. Quietly making his way to her side, he had a vague memory of lying in the bed beside her. Of his arm holding her to him, his lips brushing her cheek. Watching her sleep, he ached to take her in his arms and bury his head between her breasts. To feel the beat of her heart, to kiss away the frown from her forehead and take up where he may have left off.

Cool it, he told himself one more time. Pretend husband or not, he and Emily were practically strangers, weren't they?

He dropped onto the edge of the bed and tried to remember the past few days.

The sequence of events was almost unbelievable, even to a guy who had been part of them. To begin with, Emily's continued insistence he was the man she'd bid for and won at the bachelor's auction was the most mind-boggling thought of all.

Recalling Emily's reasons for bidding on him made him smile. Dangerous? No way. He liked to think of himself as a strong man with a heart. Still, being called ''dangerous'' was an ego builder. Thank goodness Emily hadn't chosen a really dangerous man. Otherwise, she might not be here sleeping peacefully with him watching over her.

As if he'd spoken his thoughts aloud, Emily stirred, opened her eye and met T.J.'s interested gaze. A damp lock of hair fell over his forehead. His shirt was partially unbuttoned and gave her a glimpse of his muscled chest where drops of water lingered. The masculine scent of shaving lotion clung to him. The pulse that throbbed at his neck spoke of his thoughts. She felt the accelerated beat of her heart.

"Thank goodness it's only you!" she said. "I must have fallen asleep. For a moment I didn't know where I was or who you were." She slid out of bed, tugged at her neckline and wiggled her dress back into place. "After a night like last night, I would have thought you'd still be asleep."

"Nope, all cured," he assured her cheerfully. "All cured, cleaned up and ready to talk."

It wasn't only his gaze that was making Emily uneasy. It was trying, without much success, to concentrate on something less sensuous than T.J., his handsome appearance and the twinkle in his eyes. After being jilted, sensuous thoughts should have been the last thing on her mind.

It was time to do something to take her mind off T.J.'s sexy appearance and concentrate on something more earthly. "Hungry? How about the coffee shop downstairs?"

He seemed to hesitate before he shrugged. "Great. I'm as empty as a drum and as hungry as a bear."

"Sure," Emily replied. T.J.'s feet might be bare, his clothes wrinkled, but with his innate sex appeal, the coffee shop was a lot safer than a cozy meal for two courtesy of room service. "Why don't you finish dressing while I freshen up?"

After a glance behind her to make sure he was

strong enough to navigate by himself, she headed for a sweater to cover her suddenly too low neckline.

In the elevator, Emily felt as if T.J.'s gaze singed her skin through her sweater. After spending a memorable twenty-four hours in his company, she could understand why she'd chosen him for a husband at the charity auction. And why she'd been so carried away by his persona that she hadn't stopped to realize a mere photograph wouldn't have been enough to convince the lawyer T.J. was her husband.

The ride to the crowded lobby in the closed elevator didn't help much, either. While T.J. whistled under his breath, her heart was racing. When they finally reached the lobby, after several stops, she sighed in relief.

They found the coffee shop largely empty. The hostess remarked that it was too late for lunch and too early for dinner. "No problem," T.J. replied, "we're here for breakfast."

To Emily's chagrin, the hostess smiled knowingly.

T.J. chose a table in a quiet corner, partially hidden from view by a large ficus tree. The hotel's tropical gardens were visible through a large picture window. "Mind if we sit here out of the way of traffic? It will give us a chance to talk."

"Not at all," Emily answered with a smile. Talking would take her mind off the way T.J.'s clear blue eyes were affecting her. How could she ever have believed that though they had been strangers when they met, they would still be strangers when they parted? "I may not have told you before, but I'm a librarian by profession. I'm used to quiet surroundings."

Her companion looked interested. "What else should I know about you, Miss Holmes?"

Emily folded her paper napkin in neat squares. She was a private person by nature and from what she remembered about last night, T.J. already knew more about her than she cared for him to know. "Why would you want to know anything else?"

"Because I'm here to help you."

She gazed at him warily. The kind of help she needed didn't come with killer smiles and kisses. "What kind of help, exactly?"

He looked around for the waitress. "I'll tell you as soon as I get a decent cup of very hot and black coffee."

Emily shrugged and turned her attention to the yellow and white daffodils in a blue glass vase on the table. Spring flowers that reminded her of the garden she'd planted at her aunt's cottage one summer. Those days were gone, and the cottage where she'd spent so many happy days would soon be gone, too.

She raised her eyes in time to see T.J.'s inquiring look. She couldn't tell him she'd been thinking about the cottage on her aunt's property and how much she missed her aunt. Not when she was asking him to help her gain her inheritance only to sell it. It wasn't the money she was interested in—she would have loved to move into the cottage. She belonged in Placerville, she told herself. In the position she'd worked years to earn. But not until she made her dream of visiting Italy come true.

The waitress arrived to take their orders.

"Just coffee and toast for me, please."

"Are you sure that that's all?" T.J. eyed her with concern. "In my family, if you didn't eat, it meant you were sick."

"I'm just tired and anxious, I guess." Emily smiled and reached in her purse for the roll of peppermints.

T.J. knew better. She was stressed-out over having to confront Daniels and worn-out from a night of caring for him. He offered up the menus to the waitress. "Are you sure you don't want anything else, Em?"

"Maybe a small fruit salad," she agreed.

"I'll have bacon and eggs over easy. Hash browns and a short stack. Coffee too, black."

Emily waited until the waitress left. No way was she going to bare her thoughts with an audience. "I'm sure I'll feel better when this is over. You said you wanted to talk?"

T.J. hesitated for a moment, then plunged in. He'd come this far, and it was no time to retreat. "I wanted to discuss your aunt's will. But first, if you won't think I'm getting too personal, I'm curious about a few things.''

''Such as?''

''For one thing,'' he began hesitantly, trying to gauge Emily's reaction to his intrusion into her private life. ''Why have you gone along with the marriage clause in your aunt's will? From the little I know about women, most would have contested the will right away.'' When she didn't answer, he gazed at her quizzically. If she was going to tell him to mind his own business, now was the time. He hoped not. Emily was becoming more interesting every day.

''Maybe it's because I'm not most women,'' she finally answered. ''Besides, I'd known about the clause for some time before she died. My aunt often told me she hoped I'd marry and have a family of my own.''

Her answer took T.J. by surprise. ''And it never bothered you? Even after Daniels told you about the marriage clause?''

''No,'' she answered. ''After my uncle was killed in a car accident, my aunt never remarried. I only visited during the summers before I went away to college. Unfortunately, her last years were spent in a convalescent home. I knew Aunt Emily must have wanted my life to be different than hers.''

''I guess that accounts for the condition of the

property," T.J. said thoughtfully. "After you told me about the cottage, I couldn't resist swinging by to take a look before I met you again. But there is a chance the cottage could be put into shape. How about giving me a chance to restore it for you so you can live there?"

"It's impossible. I work in Placerville and my mother lives nearby." She pushed away her coffee cup, wiped her lips with the paper napkin.

"So you intend to sell it?"

"I'm afraid so. That is, if I can find a buyer."

"You're looking at one," T.J. replied. "The opportunity to restore the cottage is something I'd hate to miss. That is, if you're sure you want to sell."

"It's not mine to sell, at least not yet," Emily answered as the waitress served the rest of their breakfast. "Ask me again later."

"You can count on it," T.J. agreed. "But back to your aunt's will. Why didn't you try to change her mind when you got older?"

"It didn't matter. I was already engaged to Sean Foster, had been for several years. I didn't dream there was going to be a problem." Her smile was ironic, but he could sense her unhappiness under the wall of indifference she'd woven around her.

"Ah, yes, I remember you told me you'd been engaged." To her obvious discomfiture, T.J.'s gaze swept her and lingered on the jade charm she wore around her neck. "The guy must have been out of his mind to break up with you."

She shrugged. "It seems Sean found greener pastures." When T.J. raised a questioning eyebrow, she added wryly, "A woman with money."

T.J. dug into his bacon and eggs. Across the table, as if food were the last thing on her mind, Emily toyed with her fresh fruit plate. She had his attention when she nibbled at a ripe strawberry and ran her tongue over her lips to catch the juice. Mesmerized, he couldn't help wishing he could be the one to kiss the juice from her lips.

Their waitress passed by and looked at T.J.'s plate. "Something wrong with the food?"

"No," he replied, surprised to discover he hadn't eaten much. "I guess I wasn't as hungry as I thought I was." He was hungry all right, but it wasn't for bacon and eggs. He lifted his empty coffee cup. "How about a refill?"

"Too bad the guy didn't hang around long enough to find out about your inheritance," T.J. said when the waitress moved on. "He might have changed his mind."

"I'm glad he didn't," Emily retorted. "I wanted a husband who would stick by me, rich or poor. I wanted to start a family, he didn't. As soon as I discovered Sean had dollar bills in place of a heart, I knew I never would have been able to trust him, let alone depend on him to become a part of my life.

After he left, I discovered I was glad to see the last of him.''

''And that's where the auction idea came in,'' T.J. added with an understanding smile. ''What would you have done if you hadn't won me?''

Emily airily dismissed his question. ''A man is a man. I would have picked someone else.''

''Emily Holmes,'' he answered with a hand over his heart. ''You wound me deeply. And here I thought you bid on me because I was the only man for you.''

Emily smothered a reply. T.J. had unwittingly hit the nail right on the head. At the time, she *had* thought he was the only man for her, even if it had been a different reason. After the way she was beginning to feel about him, he still might have been the right man if their paths had crossed under different circumstances. ''Although winning you hasn't done me much good, has it?''

T.J. drained his cup and winked. ''Em, brace yourself. I think you're in for a surprise.''

''A good one, I hope,'' she answered, brushing toast crumbs from her lap. ''I'm not sure I can take much more of this.''

The waitress arrived and smiled at T.J. ''Will there be anything else?''

''Not for me, thanks. Emily?''

''No, thanks,'' Emily answered. ''I'd much rather get on with the surprise.''

With a lingering look at T.J., the waitress left a check. Emily smothered a remark. She obviously wasn't the only woman taken by T.J.'s masculine charms.

"In a minute." T.J. felt the overwhelming urge to stand up and stretch. "If you don't mind, I've got to get my sea legs, or I'm afraid I'll wind up back in bed. Lazing around without working isn't like me. How about going for a walk?"

Emily looked doubtful. "Are you sure you're up to it?"

T.J. thought about the hotel gardens and the pool he'd seen the day he'd picked Emily up to visit Daniels. He thought about his impulsive public kiss on a busy thoroughfare. The surprising way she'd responded and how he wanted to kiss her now in a more intimate setting. A setting where they would be surrounded by the perfumed scent of flowers instead of carbon monoxide.

He'd have to pass. He'd promised Emily a surprise and he had to deliver.

"I'm sure," he answered. He picked up the check and dropped a large tip. "Let's go."

"I have to apologize for not telling you this before I passed out," he began as they strolled along meandering paths to the pool. "I should have told you I've had enough experience with the transfer of property titles in my building restoration business to know that the marriage clause in your aunt's will doesn't have a prayer of holding up. I spoke to a couple of people before I came over, and they agreed.''

Emily stopped short. ''You're not a lawyer, too, are you?''

''No, but we can hire a darn good one,'' T.J. said, and grinned. ''Noel Braude is a wealth of information. If it's okay with you, I'd like to get him involved in the case.''

''That would be wonderful,'' she answered with a sigh, ''but I'm afraid I don't have the money to pay him. That's probably the biggest reason I tried to settle everything by myself.''

T.J. wanted to kick himself at the troubled look that came into Emily's eyes. He should have remembered Emily had said she'd spent most of her ready money on buying him. He should have told her what he found out before he'd almost passed out at Emily's feet. All that sun must have softened his brain.

''Not to worry, Em. The visit won't cost you a dime. Like I said, Noel is on a retainer anyway. He'll be glad to help out.''

Emily's heart skipped a beat. There it was again, ''Em.'' The pet name he used at such odd moments. A name that warmed her heart and reminded her of the two people in her life who had truly loved her for herself. ''What would I have to do?''

T.J. smiled down at her. ''Not much, just trust me to do the right thing.''

Trust. Emily cringed inside. After her experience with Sean, trusting a man to do the right thing, let alone relying on a man she'd only known for a few days, wasn't going to be easy.

They'd stopped at a corner of the kidney-sized pool. Stirred by a gentle breeze, a shimmering reflection of palm trees appeared on its surface. The scent of orange blossoms filled the air. To add to the romantic ambience, soft music wafted through the air from speakers hidden in the background.

T.J. smothered a sigh. Standing beside the pool with Emily close to his side seemed so right, he didn't want the moment to end. Against a background of lavender and rose-colored oleander bushes, she looked lovelier than ever. Everything about Emily was perfect, he mused thoughtfully, the way she walked, the way she talked, the way her expressive eyes spoke for her.

He was tempted to throw caution to the wind, take her in his arms and kiss her until the growing need within him was satisfied. To taste her lips and inhale the scent of strawberries. To relive that first impulsive kiss and, above all, to make time stand still.

He couldn't, not after he'd asked her to trust him. And not after he remembered it might be the right place but the wrong time for romance in their lives. Especially his.

A swimmer dove into the pool and sent drops of water into the air. The cold spray was just what he

needed to break his mellow mood, T.J. thought ruefully as he wiped it from his forehead. There was
the more important matter of Emily's inheritance to
take care of. He had to reconcile his attraction to
her.

HIS LAWYER'S OFFICE was on the tenth floor of the
Zenith Building in the Wilshire Boulevard corridor.
His lawyer, the Braude of Weinstein, Braude and
Collins came out to greet them as soon as Emily and
T.J. were announced. "Took your time to get here,
didn't you?"

T.J. scowled. Unless his friend was gifted with a
sixth sense, Noel couldn't possibly have known he
was coming. "How did you know I was on my
way?"

"Your dad, bless him. We had a few contracts to
go over this morning, and he filled me in on what's
going on. I figured you'd turn up here today." He
shook hands with T.J. "Mind introducing me to
your lady?"

"Sorry. Emily, this is Noel, the Braude in the
partnership. Emily is Miss Holmes to you," he
added, into Noel's broad grin. Behind Emily's back,
he mouthed a request that Noel call him T.J. instead
of Tom. Oddly enough, T.J. wasn't too happy to
make the introduction. Like Tim, Noel had a reputation as a lady's man.

As they sat down. T.J. briefly wondered just how

much filling in about Emily and her problem his father had done. The auction? The case of the mistaken identity?

With the way things were going, he'd be lucky to resolve Emily's inheritance and send her on her way without giving away his true identity. He'd tried to be up-front with her at the time of their meeting, hadn't he? She hadn't believed him then, and she hadn't mentioned it since. Still, he was treading on thin ice.

If the truth came out now, she was sure to think he had been playing a game at her expense.

Impossible! No matter how he felt about her selling her property and the possibility the cottage might be torn down, Emily needed her inheritance more than she needed to know the truth about his identity.

"Now, from the way I understand it, Miss Holmes," Noel began, "your aunt's will states you have to be a married woman in order to inherit her estate?"

Emily nodded. "Yes, and please call me Emily."

Noel made a notation on a yellow legal pad. "Thank you. Please call me Noel. Now, are there any other possible beneficiaries to the estate? A parent perhaps?"

"No," Emily answered. "My paternal grandfather was my Aunt Emily's brother. And I'm an only child of his only child, my father. I'm afraid we were a small family.''

''The blood tie makes it easier, Emily.'' Noel made another notation, sat back in his chair and smiled his satisfaction. ''According to the probate laws of the State of California, and as long as there are no other possible legatees, in this instance the entire inheritance passes to you as the only surviving heir. Married or not.''

Emily gasped. ''I was sure Daniels had something to hide. But why would he tell me a lie?''

''Because the man probably had a motive of his own. While you are the legal heir in this case, he makes money another way. Under California law, where there is no will, or no clear legatees, ownership of an estate passes to the state. Daniels, or someone like him, manages to get himself appointed as executor. He not only gets a fee, it then becomes possible for him to buy the estate for himself after taxes are paid. In your case, Emily, you're your aunt's only surviving blood relative, so it's not germane.''

''So why did he pick on me?''

''My guess is Daniels thinks he can get you out of the picture by claiming you're not a legal heir. Or at least, to intimidate you into paying him a large fee for getting the estate settled in your favor.''

T.J. turned a pleased smile on Emily. ''Why don't you show Noel Wilbur Daniels's business card, so he can see if it's the same guy. It sounds to me as if Daniels makes a practice of preying on naive or vulnerable people.''

Emily dug in her purse, came up with the card and passed it across the desk.

"Yeah, that's the guy," Noel said after a quick look at the card. "It doesn't come as a surprise to me to find he's tried to put one over on you."

He handed back the business card. "In case you were going to ask why he hasn't been arrested for marginal practices, I'm sure Daniels has always managed to stay within the law by pushing its boundaries."

T.J. got to his feet and leaned across the desk. "Let me get this straight. The property is Emily's?"

"Sure thing," Noel responded cheerfully. "Want me to take care of Daniels?"

"No way," T.J. said firmly. "This is my show. I've got a score to settle with the man, and I can't wait."

"You might want to consider doing it without laying him out, or you might wind up in jail, T.J. I promised your dad I'd caution you against violence." Noel laughed. "The way you look now, I don't envy Daniels."

Emily rose and put a warning hand on T.J.'s arm. "Daniels said he's going to be out of town for a few days. I'm sure T.J. will have cooled off by then."

When T.J. and his lawyer exchanged knowing smiles, Emily realized she should have known better.

She glanced at T.J. and felt her heart race. She was in for trouble, for sure. And not just with Daniels.

Chapter Seven

True to his word, T.J.'s promise to help had been a
promise kept. So far, so good, Emily thought as they
waited for an elevator. It was what might come next
that worried her. To add to her distress, the magnetic
pull between her and T.J. was growing stronger by
the minute.

The mirrored doors of the elevator reflected an
attractive couple. With a start, her gaze met his in
the mirror, and she lost herself in his warm blue
eyes.

Maybe it had been the tingle that had danced up
her spine when he'd walked onstage. She just hadn't
planned on falling in love.

"You're awfully quiet, Em," T.J. murmured. "I
thought you'd be happy after Noel explained your
rights to your aunt's property. Something bothering
you?"

"Not at all, I was just thinking." She hoped he
wouldn't ask where her thoughts had taken her. Cer-

tainly not in an empty elevator with its enforced intimacy. And not when she wasn't sure of the answer.

Resolutely she stared at the gold carpet, but every inch of her skin was aware of him and the scented tang of his cool, masculine aftershave.

Her sensual reaction to T.J., when she'd seen him at the building site, had come as a surprise. Her reaction to his open shirt and suntanned muscles had been a greater surprise. After her failed engagement, she'd told herself men came in last on her most-wanted list. And yet, here she was practically joined at the hip with a man who set her mind on fire by just looking at her.

It had to be some kind of magic that was robbing her of her common sense.

The elevator halted, taking on a noisy family. She welcomed the distraction of a two-year-old waving adorable kisses. And her older brother making faces at himself in the mirrored elevator doors.

She glanced at T.J. A smile lingered on his lips, his body relaxed. He was a man comfortable in his skin. To add to her dilemma about the direction their unusual relationship seemed to be headed, her conscience began to bother her. What if he and Daniels actually squared off over her aunt's will, and he got hurt? Getting him involved was her fault.

"Perhaps we should say goodbye now," she said when the elevator reached the lobby.

He swung around and stared at her. "Where did that come from?"

She dodged the little boy racing out of the elevator. His father took off after him, but his mother stopped to apologize. "No problem," Emily smiled. She turned to T.J. "Now that your lawyer has explained my rights, I'm sure Daniels is too smart to give me any more trouble."

T.J. took Emily by the arm and held her back until the rest of the elevator cleared. Before anyone could get on, he punched the buttons that closed the door and sent the elevator back to the top floor to an empty terrace garden.

"No way are you going to see that man alone. As far as I'm concerned, I'm not through with him. He'll keep preying on innocent people if someone doesn't stop him." He looked grim and went on. "I've made up my mind that that someone is going to be me. In case you don't know me by now, I always finish what I start."

The fighting look in T.J.'s eyes told Emily she had little chance of winning the argument, but she still had to try. "So do I," she answered. "I'm twenty-eight years old, and I've been taking care of my own affairs for a long time. And that includes settling with Daniels."

If he hadn't been so taken by Emily's declaration of independence, T.J. would have been amused by two hardheaded, well-meaning people behaving like dogs arguing over the same bone.

Not that he questioned Emily's effectiveness as a librarian. He didn't. It was just too bad she didn't realize a library was a quiet, secluded place where she was on her own turf. Being street smart was something else.

He watched her lean over to smell a gardenia. Her auburn hair swung forward, hiding her face. His gaze lingered on the soft pale skin at her throat. As if suddenly aware of his gaze, she turned back to challenge him with a defiant look.

He eyed her resolute expression, but in no way did he intend to back off. Allowing Emily to tackle Daniels by herself would be tantamount to sending her into the lion's den with predictable results. His conscience and his growing awareness of Emily's attraction wouldn't let him.

"Real or not, I'm in for the duration," he answered amiably. He threw his arm around her shoulder and tried to lighten up the moment. "Come on, Em. The way I was raised, men take care of their wives. I signed up to be your husband, and I intend to remain your husband until this is over."

No sooner had he announced he was Emily's husband than T.J. began to wish he hadn't been so noble. He had to remember his natural mother had given him and his brother away like unwanted gifts. Based on that unhappy memory, and with Emily's avowed wanderlust, she didn't fill the requirements he had in mind for a wife. Not when she reminded him of his mother. No matter how much he was attracted to her.

Considering how he felt about marriage, he should have referred to himself as a friend. *Friendship* would have been a better operative word. When the right time came, he would have room to gracefully maneuver his way out of the role his brother had thrust on him.

Surprised at the road his thoughts were taking, he caught the inquiring look in Emily's intriguing hazel eyes. If he really thought of himself as her friend, he asked himself, why was his arm still around her shoulders? And why did he want to ask her not to leave at the same time she was trying to say goodbye? And why was the need to feel her lips under his one more time robbing him of the little common sense he had left?

When T.J. reached to brush her cheek with the tip of his forefinger before he kissed her, Emily's resolve to send him away vanished into the warm breeze. Sean's kisses had never been like this. This was a kiss of a man who was real, genuine. A man who cared about her.

His touch was magical, warm and gentle, his breath a sigh against her cheek. When his lips met hers, she became lost in a velvet haze of desire. She drank in T.J.'s kiss with a hunger she'd never known she possessed and returned it with all the stored-up passion in her. If it was wrong, she didn't care. In his embrace, she forgot that she'd tried to send him away, couldn't even remember why she'd wanted to.

Somewhere in the back of her mind, she was aware there had been a question in T.J.'s eyes before he kissed her. Was it the same question that lingered in the back of her mind? Were they wise to let emotion get in the way of rational thought?

Considering how they had met and that they would soon part, were they doing the right thing in going beyond a business agreement?

She'd read somewhere that danger was an aphrodisiac. With a shock, she realized it was true. Her reaction to T.J.'s sensuous persona was a rush of excitement, a desire to lose herself in the male mystery she'd seen in his eyes.

Whatever the reason behind the rush of passion she was experiencing, she mused as she leaned into his embrace, there was no place she'd rather have been than here in his arms.

When Emily made no move to pull out of his embrace, T.J. told himself he'd meant to kiss her only once, and as a test. Just once, to satisfy the growing hunger that had exploded within him. Instead, her fervent response drew him to a place where questions didn't require an answer. A place where two people acknowledged how they felt about each other in the most natural of ways.

Throwing caution to the winds, he deepened the kiss, held her so close he could feel the beat of her heart. To his pleasure, her kiss tasted of an intriguing combination of mint and strawberries.

He'd meant only to taste, to remain firm in his resolve to move on when he'd helped Emily get her heart's desire. Instead, these moments with her in his arms was all he seemed to care about. He told himself that tomorrow would have to take care of itself.

When Emily finally broke away and gently fingered the lock of hair that fell into his eyes, he read a tenderness, a look of genuine affection, in her gaze. His heart thundered, his senses whirled, mental warning bells rang. Was her touch an omen? A warning he was pushing boundaries? Boundaries he'd set for himself?

Emily was the forever type no matter what plans she'd made for herself. He wasn't, at least, not yet. She was the type he'd vowed to stay away from. But how to tell her the truth after kissing her like this without looking like a fool? He swallowed hard and cursed himself for biting off more than he could chew.

Shaken by the sound of faraway church bells measuring the time, T.J. swallowed hard and met

Emily's eyes. "I'm sorry, Em, I probably shouldn't have done that."

For a moment, she looked shaken; her bewildered expression tore at him. How could she believe him, or even trust him when he kissed her one moment and apologized the next? He was relieved when she smiled faintly and put a finger against his lips.

"There's nothing to be sorry for. It was just a goodbye kiss, wasn't it?"

He couldn't come up with an answer. Maybe she was right. Maybe, in this crazy world he'd found himself since he'd met up with Emily, this *was* the way to say goodbye. No. He had to be honest with himself. If he kept this up, he would be saying a lot of things and none of them would be a goodbye.

He resisted the temptation to ignore the sound of the church bells, to forget precious time was passing. He told himself this was not the time and the place for embraces that had no chance of going anywhere. For two people who had nothing in common but an auction receipt, things were getting out of hand.

He'd vowed not to marry until he found a woman who was a "keeper." A woman who would love him, stick by him and the children they would have. A woman who would help create happy memories for their children to cherish, not the memories of being left that still haunted his dreams.

He had to be sure Emily was that woman. That

she hadn't meant she wanted to pursue a dream that didn't include him.

If that wasn't reason enough for him to cool it, she was apparently convinced he was his brother, Tim. If she ever had to face the truth, it would be over with them, anyway. Love had to be based on trust. He knew that as surely as he knew the sun would rise in the morning and set in the evening.

"Why don't I see you back to the hotel so you can get some rest," he finally said into the silence that had fallen between them. He rang for the elevator. "When I think back on the condition I was in last night, I realize I must have given you a bad time."

Emily's smile faded. "No rougher than yours," she said quietly. She stiffened and moved away. "You look as if you could use some rest, too."

"Guess so." He mentally kicked himself for taking the smile from her face. "At any rate," he went on, "it's time I checked in with my foreman, Duke. I wouldn't want him to think I've fallen off the face of the earth. There's still work to be done on the fire station." He took a deep breath as the elevator door opened. "So, back to the hotel?"

"Only for another day or two." She shrugged helplessly. "I'm afraid I used up most of my ready cash at the auction. If Daniels doesn't come back soon, I'll have to max out my credit card."

T.J. was tempted to take her home to stay with

him for the duration, but instinct told him he would be courting trouble. That was the important thing he had to remember. No matter how strongly he was attracted to Emily, and no matter how obligated he felt to go on helping her with the lawyer, he wasn't ready to continue to be a bridegroom, real or otherwise.

"Tell you what," he said, "I know a pretty good bed-and-breakfast down near the beach. Several of my clients have stayed there while we renovated their homes. I'm sure you'd be welcome there until the estate is settled."

Emily looked uncertain. "I'm not sure I can afford it. It all depends on what they charge."

"It's in your ballpark," he assured her. He knew better than to offer to help her. She was an independent and proud woman. He could tell Emily wasn't used to taking favors, but he felt he owed her.

Hell, she'd paid three hundred and fifty dollars for his brother, hadn't she? The way he looked at it, since Tim had run out on her, she was entitled to a refund. His own services were on the house.

As they walked to his car, he could sense he hadn't convinced Emily to take him up on his offer to find a less expensive place to live. "I'll call and make a reservation for you at the Hollisters' when we get back to the hotel."

Emily nodded reluctantly. Not only because of the

unexpected expense caused by Daniels's departure, but because it looked as if T.J. would be around only for a little while longer.

There was the way he'd started calling her Em.

He couldn't possibly know how much the nickname meant to her. If he kept calling her Em, he would surely break her heart before they were through.

Independence was fine, but the thought of never seeing T.J. again after her inheritance was settled left her with a hollow feeling.

"A gentleman left a message for you, Miss Holmes," the desk clerk announced when Emily asked for her key. He handed her an envelope. "The message is inside," he explained. "We keep all of our guests' messages confidential."

A gentleman? Since the only people who knew where she was staying outside of T.J. were Daniels and her mother, Emily's heart began to beat like a drum. The lawyer's return meant T.J. would leave, and she would never see him again.

"I'm back!" T.J.'s cheerful voice sounded as he came up behind her. "For a time I wasn't sure I'd driven here by myself or if it was all a bad dream. I'll never know how I managed to get here in the first place without getting in an accident." He sobered when he saw her troubled expression and noticed the envelope in her hand. "Bad news?"

"I don't know," she replied, torn between her

warm memories of spending part of last night in
T.J.'s arms and her dread of finding out what was
in the envelope. "I haven't had a chance to look at
the message. I'm not even sure who it's from."

"You'll never know until you open it, will you?"
T.J. led her to a secluded corner of the lobby. "This
spot ought to be private enough. Why don't you take
a deep breath and go for it?" He paused, as if uncertain whether or not to stay. "I'll wait for you over
by the pool, but feel free to call me if you need or
want me."

Need him? Maybe not, she thought as she
watched him saunter away with that sensuous lope
of his. Want him? Heaven help her; for all the good
wanting him would do her, she did. She knew she
would always want him, even after he'd gone his
own way. To hold her, to make love to her, to finish
what they'd started.

The question was did he want her?

From the first moment they'd met, she'd sensed
he couldn't make up his mind what to do about her
or with her. Even after he'd kissed her in the way
of a man who desires a woman, she still didn't know
where she stood with him.

She waited until T.J. disappeared through the door
and into the hotel gardens and wished with all her
heart she could ignore the message and go after him.

With a sigh, she tore open the envelope and read

the message that left her as cold as if she'd been
plunged into a bath of ice-cold water.

The message was from Sean Foster, her ex-fiancé.
The last person she wanted to hear from, let alone
ever see again. And yet, as she studied Sean's familiar handwriting, she felt a stab in her heart. She'd
built a dream of a home and children into their relationship before he walked away. Maybe it was impossible to forget your first love.

She crushed the slip of paper into a tight ball and
threw it into a nearby container. She didn't want to
see Sean, and suddenly realized she didn't want to
see T.J. again, either. Her experience with both men
had taught her a hard lesson. There wasn't a man
alive she could trust to want her for herself.

With a quick glance around the lobby, she decided now was her chance to check out before either
man appeared. If she intended to take charge of her
life, the time was now.

"Emily, sweetheart!" Emily froze at the sound of
Sean's familiar voice, the last voice she wanted to
hear. She swung around.

Caught in a corner of the lobby, there was no way
to escape him. Seeing him again brought back memories she fought hard to forget. "Hello, Sean. What
are you doing here? How did you find me?"

He dropped his arms, but she knew him well
enough to recognize the proprietary look in his eyes.
As if he'd sensed any lingering sentiment she might

feel for him, he acted as if she still belonged to him. If he'd taken the trouble to try to understand her and the way she might feel about his desertion, he would have known she wasn't the same woman he'd walked away from.

"I've seen the light, Emily, and I wanted to start over," he answered. "Unfortunately, by the time I realized how wrong I was to leave you for Stella Morgan, you'd already left town."

Emily backed away. "I asked you how you knew where to find me?"

"I would have searched everywhere for you, sweetheart," he assured her, turning up the brilliant false smile that had fooled her three years ago. "Luckily, my aunt told me she ran into your mother at the beauty parlor and your mother mentioned you were down here."

He sounded sincere, even repentant, but Emily knew better. His turnaround was too convenient. Now that she had objective eyes to see the truth of their relationship, she wondered if Sean had ever really cared for her. Or if she'd been a convenient woman to romance while he waited for a woman with money like Stella to come along. Meeting his false smile, she finally knew what kind of man Sean was. Stella hadn't been as wealthy as he'd believed her to be. She could never reconcile with Sean.

She hardened her heart. He'd fooled her once, and he wasn't going to fool her twice. "Was that before or after my mother told your aunt why I'm in Los Angeles?''

He shrugged, the answer in his eyes. ''Come on, Emily. I've told you I'm sorry I was such a jerk. I'm here now, that's what counts. We loved each other before, so how about getting together again?''

Emily already knew the answer. Old memories might linger, but sometimes they belonged in the past. She had to get rid of him, and now. By the time he showed up again, she'd be long gone. ''Why don't you call me tomorrow. We'll talk about it then.'' Her heart skipped a beat at the lie.

A faint flush covered his face, but he shrugged. ''If that's what it takes, I'm game. I'm staying with a friend in the valley, but I'll get in touch with you first thing in the morning.'' He paused. ''But first, here's something for you to remember me by.'' Before Emily could react, he took her in his arms and kissed her.

Across the lobby, T.J. froze in his tracks. Emily, the woman he'd grown to admire for her honesty, was caught in the passionate embrace of a man. He couldn't believe his eyes, until he remembered the envelope she'd been holding when he left her a few moments ago. Her ex-fiancé? Had the guy come back to take up where they'd left off?

She must have welcomed the kiss, or she would have called for help by now. A pang of jealousy shot through him. He started toward her, then stopped. Emily had reminded him she intended to take charge of her life, hadn't she? Whomever she was kissing, it was none of his business.

So much for being afraid he might break her heart.

Maybe he had it coming. He'd never told her how grateful he was to her for taking care of him. Or taken the time to tell her his gratitude had turned into something more. It was either too late for him. Or maybe he'd never had a chance.

EMILY HURRIED to her room after promising to answer Sean's plea for a second chance in the morning. She'd already made up her mind to check out now, if only to get rid of him. She was never going to allow herself to be hurt by Sean or manipulated by T.J.—a man who waxed hot and cold until she couldn't be sure how he felt about her.

To her dismay, a second upholstered armchair had been added to the furniture in her room. The hotel doctor must have passed the word along that she and T.J. were newlyweds. A bucket of champagne on ice had been placed on a stand alongside. A floral arrangement and a basket of fresh fruit were on the small table. The only item missing was a wedding cake.

Newlyweds. Although she no longer associated the word with Sean, the description held too much pain for her to dwell on it. She hadn't fully realized until this very moment that she would have been happy to forget her dream of Italy and spend the future with T.J. If he'd really wanted her to.

She gazed at the bed where she'd spent part of the night in T.J.'s arms. And the upholstered armchair where she'd watched over him while he slept away his fever. Both vivid reminders that she'd gone beyond merely being attracted to the man. They were reminders that she'd actually begun to fall in love with him.

She started to pack the few things she'd brought with her. It was foolish to dwell on the past. She'd promised herself a chance to live a long-held dream to travel to Venice, Italy. Now that she was alone and armed with the truth to gain her inheritance, she'd do it without the man who'd stolen her heart.

Chapter Eight

"You may as well let me in, Em. I'm not going to go away."

Emily opened the hotel door to T.J. "How on earth did you find me?"

"When I found out you'd moved, I went to Daniels's office. Seems you left a forwarding address with his secretary. But more to the point, why did you check in here instead of letting me take you to Hollisters'?"

Emily hesitated. There was no way she could tell him that after Sean had appeared she'd sworn off men for the duration, she was almost broke. "I wanted to be alone for a while to think things over. The doorman at the Beaumont told me about this hotel. It's not only convenient, it's inexpensive."

"Inexpensive is right," he answered with a glance over her shoulder at the worn carpet, the sagging window blinds and a narrow bed covered with a fading blanket. Emily deserved more. If he had his way, she would be sleeping on silken sheets in a room filled with furniture fit for a queen.

Emily wasn't surprised to hear T.J. had been persistent in trying to find her. He had enough self-assurance for two men, let alone one. To add to his appeal, just by looking at her, he made a woman feel wanted. She'd caught the message from the moment she'd laid eyes on him working alongside his crew at the building site.

There probably wasn't a woman alive who wasn't susceptible to his killer smile.

In his tan slacks, crisply pressed white shirt and brown jacket, he looked as if he'd stepped off the cover of a magazine. To add to his charm, the shock of hair that persisted in hanging over his brow lent him a roguish look. The same look that had attracted her to him and that had evidently done a number on Daniels's secretary. Poor woman, she hadn't had a chance.

He looked so pleased with himself, she sensed the secretary had given him more than an address. "What else did she give you?"

"I told Maggie you needed the key to your aunt's cottage. Since she'd seen us together, I guess she made the assumption we were married."

Emily was taken aback. "Too bad Daniels didn't buy the charade as well as his secretary."

"To tell the truth, I don't think Maggie likes Daniels any better than we do." T.J. glanced over Emily's shoulder. "Are you alone, or is someone here with you?"

Emily frowned at the intimate question. "I'm alone. Why?"

"The last time I saw you, you were having a reunion with some guy."

Emily thought back to when T.J. had left her alone so she could read Sean's message. She'd sent Sean away and hadn't wanted to see him again, but she'd still been puzzled when T.J. hadn't come back before she checked out of the Beaumont. Now she knew why. He'd been jealous.

"That was Sean, my ex-fiancé." Embarrassed that T.J. had seen her in Sean's arms after telling him Sean had jilted her, she opened the door. "If you want to talk, you might as well do it inside instead of out in the hall." She closed the door behind him. "Sean had the idea we would get together again, but I managed to put him off. If you'd have stuck around long enough, you would have seen him leave."

"It doesn't matter," T.J. replied. He tried not to let his relief show. But it did matter to him who Emily kissed. He couldn't bring himself to confess he'd felt a pang of jealousy when he'd seen Sean grab her and kiss her."

"I saw you, but when you didn't call for help, I figured you had to know the guy." He gazed into Emily's eyes and told her the first direct lie he'd ever told her but not that it had taken all his will-power to turn on his heel and leave her with Sean. "After all, it's none of my business whom you kiss."

"It isn't? Then what are you doing here?"

Emily's eyes reflected her unhappiness. He wanted to tell her it mattered. He wanted to tell her he didn't want her to kiss anyone but him. He couldn't bring himself to say the words her eyes told him she wanted to hear.

Yesterday, he'd sworn to forget her. To chalk her up as another woman with an itchy foot, the kind he'd avoided like the plague. Instead, she drew him in like a magnet.

"I came to take you to check out the cottage. If it's habitable, I figured you might want to stay there. What the heck, it's rent free."

The light faded from her eyes. He wanted to kick himself, but he was afraid to finish what he'd started back in the elevator yesterday.

Emily hesitated. "What about Daniels? What will he do when he finds out I've moved in?"

"Under the circumstances, he hasn't a prayer of stopping you," T.J. answered. "If he tries, he'll have to answer to me. So, if you're game, why don't you get a sweater, and we'll check out the cottage?"

Emily still hesitated. He watched while she glanced around the threadbare room, struggling to make up her mind. "I wouldn't want you to get into trouble because of me."

"I'm not expecting any trouble, Em. I'm your friend. You can trust me."

Friend. He hadn't seriously thought of Emily in terms of more than friendship until now. He cared about her in ways he'd never thought he'd feel. Maybe that's what real love was all about, he mused while Emily took a sweater out of her suitcase and looked around the room. Caring for someone more than you cared for yourself.

He gazed at Emily's long, navy-blue skirt, matching sweater and sheer white silk blouse. She looked lost, vulnerable, and it was his fault. He felt a jolt of guilt, mixed with desire shoot through him. If he got any closer, emotionally, to Emily, he'd fall in love for sure.

"Ready? Let's go see if the cottage is in any shape for you to live in."

"What happens if Daniels comes back and finds us there?"

He gazed at her with unrepentant good humor. "Maggie's promised to call me and warn me."

Emily sighed and gave in.

When they reached Venice, moonlight and stars were reflected off the water in the canal that fronted the cottage. Warm summer breezes sent the fresh, salty scent of the ocean through the air. Seagulls flew overhead and dove into the ocean to catch a meal before sweeping off over the horizon.

"I've felt as though I'm coming home every time

I come here," Emily said softly. When T.J. gazed down at her, she motioned to the cottage, a dreamy look in her eyes. "You might think I'm being fanciful, but I can still hear Aunt Emily's welcoming voice. I can smell my favorite shortbread cookies she always had ready for me. I even feel the warmth of her welcoming arms."

She sighed and stood gazing at the white weathered cottage that glimmered in the dusk. "I've felt more loved here than anywhere else in my life."

"Then, stay here, Em," he said impulsively. He put his arm around her and drew her close. "It sounds as if this is where you belong."

"I wish I could, but I'm afraid it's not practical." Hand in hand, they walked along the canal pathway to the porch of the silent cottage. "I'm Placerville's head librarian. I've taken a leave of absence for three months, but I can't just walk away for good. And there's my mother who lives in Placerville. Outside of some cousins back East, Mom's the only relative I have left. I couldn't ask her to leave her job, her friends and come down here to start a new life at her age."

"There are libraries down here, too," T.J. replied. "In fact, there's a great one just around the corner from my apartment. I'm sure your mother can find something to do here, too."

"It's not that easy," Emily said wistfully. "Besides, there's my dream of seeing the real Venice.

My mother understands the way I feel, and I'm sure Aunt Emily would have, too."

"Venice, Italy, or Venice, California, what difference does it make?" T.J. rejoined as they walked along the canal. Knowing that it might be his last chance to persuade her to remain here long enough for him to sort out his obligations, his emotions, he put his heart and soul into his question. "I've often heard that home is where your heart is. Maybe this is the place where your dream can come true."

Emily shook her head. "I've already asked for a leave of absence, and a substitute has been hired. I've come too far to turn back now."

"Then sell the property to me," T.J. urged. "I'll restore it to its original state and take care of it just the way your aunt would have done. I'll even give you visiting privileges."

"Thank you," Emily replied. Impulsively she reached to brush his cheek with gentle fingers. "You have no idea how good it makes me feel to know someone would care for the cottage as much as I do."

T.J. wasn't too sure about how he made Emily feel, but he had a good idea of how Emily was making *him* feel. His head might be advising caution, but his body demanded more than a touch on his cheek. He wanted Emily in his arms, to taste her lips, to make her his and to hear her tell him she cared for him and would never leave him.

He had to make up his mind about the direction his own life would take, and soon, before she got away from him. He had to reconcile the way he was beginning to feel about Emily with his responsibilities. He had to remember his vow to wait for the right woman. Yet, all of his senses told him the right woman could be standing beside him, her hair shining in the moonlight, stars in her eyes. He took a deep breath. Vows be damned. He wasn't going to let another moment pass without telling her so.

''Em?'' He stopped and waited until she looked up at him expectantly before he folded her in his arms, tasted her minty sent and caressed her neck, her shoulders. ''Em,'' he repeated as he kissed the side of her throat where a pulse was beating madly and moved on to the hollow between her breasts.

Fog and a cool salt wind rolled in off the ocean. Emily clung tightly to him as if she were cold. He rubbed her shoulders, opened his jacket and closed it around them. His body heat must have made a difference. She closed her eyes and leaned against his chest.

His thoughts turned to the way she'd looked lying in bed the other night, fast asleep. And how much he'd wanted to join her there. If tonight wound up the way he hoped it would, they would soon be lying skin to skin, lips to lips. Only this time, he'd make sure he was wide-awake to show her how much he'd begun to care for her.

He ran his hands through her silken hair and marveled at the desire that swelled within him. "I can't seem to get enough of you, Em," he murmured.

Emily couldn't get enough of T.J., either. He'd started out as a stranger, but she didn't think of him as a stranger any longer. Not after the heart-stopping kisses he gave her and the strength of the arms that held her. She buried her head under his chin and tried to lose herself in the beat of his heart.

It wasn't like her to react this way to a man she scarcely knew and longed to know better. And certainly not after Sean's betrayal. The magic between them was more real than she could explain, even to herself.

She was sure no other man but T.J. could have understood the strong bond that still existed between her and the cottage. Or could have connected to that bond himself.

Was it the cottage and the nostalgic memories it brought back that were making her want him with every beat of her heart?

A foghorn blew in the distance, a lonely sound that awakened her to the truth. Tonight might be only a temporary stop on the road to realizing a dream.

She shifted in T.J.'s arms. He hadn't told her he loved her in so many words. She had to be practical and make a decision—her growing love for T.J., or the cottage and the real world waited for her.

T.J. reluctantly let her go. "Come on, Em, maybe we'd better check on the cottage before the night is over. I want to make sure it's okay for you to stay here for a few days."

In no hurry to awaken any more memories, Emily held back. "It's awfully dark in there. Did you remember to bring a flashlight?"

"No, something better than that," he assured her with his arm around her shoulder. "After I got the key from Daniels's secretary, I had the utilities turned on."

"You what?" Emily knew T.J. was a decision maker, but this time she was afraid he'd gone too far.

"I had the utilities turned on," he repeated with the killer smile that almost made her weep. "And, furthermore, I used Daniels's name."

Horrified, Emily stared wide-eyed at T.J. "You didn't!"

"I did," he answered with a shrug. "After all, if he's the executor of the estate, he should expect to have a few expenses."

Emily threw in the towel. T.J. looked so pleased with himself she didn't have the heart to remind him not to put himself in harm's way for her sake.

He led the way to the porch, pulled aside honeysuckle vines that framed the door, and fit the key into the lock. After a gentle push, the door swung open, and she followed him into a small, silent living room. He flipped on the light switch to reveal furniture covered with dusty sheets,

A window seat covered with wine velvet cushions backed by a large picture window overlooked the canal and the ornate concrete bridge outside. Wine colored velvet drapes partially hid the seat. Family photographs still hung on the walls, their frames heavy with dust. An ancient Kimball piano took up one wall. A metronome sat on top as if waiting for someone to sit down and play.

He gestured to the window seat. "Looks like your favorite hideaway is still here, Em."

Emily moved to his side to finger the velvet drapes. "I used to make this my own little world by spending hours in here reading behind the closed drapes. After I borrowed a library book on the real Venice, I was hooked. From then on, I dreamed of going to Italy and painting the buildings and the canals."

She gestured to a charcoal drawing of an ornate concrete bridge crossing a canal. "I used to paint a great deal. I drew that picture when I was twelve by using the bridge outside as a model. You'll probably laugh at me, but when I was little, I thought dragons and monsters lived on the other side of the bridge."

"You did!"

"I'm afraid I did. In all the years I came here to visit, I never once crossed over that bridge. I was too afraid of what I'd find."

"Never? Not even with your aunt?"

"Never," she said with a smile. "I guess the older I get, the less I know just which of those many dreams of mine were real."

T.J. had already begun to suspect Emily's adult dreams had turned into looking for something besides going to Italy. He had his own dreams to reconcile with reality and hadn't gotten there yet. But one thing for sure, the more Emily told him of her childhood, the more he fell in love with the child in her. And the lovely woman she'd become.

"Do you really think you can rediscover your childhood in Italy?" he asked softly, lightly brushing her cheek with his knuckles.

Emily shivered and turned her face into his hand. "It's more than that. Just what, I'm not sure. But somehow I feel something or someone is waiting for me out there somewhere. I just have to go and find it. What I *am* sure of is that my aunt would understand if I choose to sell the cottage to look."

"If you say so," T.J. answered as he turned away and checked under the dust sheets. "By the way, didn't your mother miss you when you were down here so much of the time?"

"I'm sure she must have, but my father was sick most of the time. Mom used to say that my staying here with Aunt Emily was a blessing."

"Then stay here, Em," T.J. said again. "Stay

here and maybe all your dreams, real or not, will come true.''

"You could be right, but what if they don't?" Emily turned away from the window seat and ran a finger over a dusty picture frame.

She glanced around the room. "I wish I could feel better about leaving all of this behind or selling it.''

Emily sounded so wistful, T.J. was tempted to take her back in his arms and show her the present could be every bit as good as her memories of the past. It wouldn't be fair. No way was he going to take advantage of the way the cottage and its memories had mellowed her.

"Come on," he said, taking her hand back in his. "Let's check out the rest of the house."

Sliding doors opened to a dining room with pegged oak floors. A yellow oak pedestal table with four matching chairs filled the room. The glass door panes of the built-in wall cabinets were made of priceless cut crystal. A marble mantel framed a fireplace on one wall.

T.J. was enchanted. The cottage and everything in it apparently were of a long-ago period when craftsmanship mattered. The same craftsmanship he tried to use when he was restoring vintage buildings. He knew from experience that not only the furniture, but also the interior decoration of the cottage had to be worth a small fortune.

He gazed at a large colored photograph of a

young girl and an older woman in vintage costumes hanging over the mantle. From the close resemblance, he recognized the woman had to be Emily's aunt. An older version of Emily, her features were small and delicate. Her intelligent eyes seemed to speak to him, her pepper hair was gathered in a neat pouf at the top of her head. One hand rested on the lace collar that framed her slender neck, the other rested on a little girl's shoulder. On closer inspection, he made out tiny Cécile Brunner roses pinned to the lace collar.

"You and your Aunt Emily?"

"Yes," she answered as she joined him. "I remember it was taken for my ninth birthday. My aunt made the dress of navy-blue taffeta. I thought it was the nicest present anyone had ever given me. The photographer was so pleased, he displayed a copy in his studio window. He called it 'The Two Emilys.'"

Her answer earned her another hug from T.J. "There's a kitchen, too. Right? I can't leave you here with a clear conscience unless I know you're eating properly. I worry about you, you know."

Emily was touched at his confession. "The cottage may be seventy years old, but my aunt prided herself on having a modern kitchen. I'm sure I can whip up a meal or two while I'm here."

"Good," he answered. "Now, to the bedrooms."

Emily led him down a short hall and paused in

front of a closed door. "This is my aunt's room."
After a pause she started to move on.

"Aren't you going to look inside?" T.J. lingered
at the door and looked surprised when she shook her
head.

"I can't, I just can't. At least, not right now. I
miss my aunt so much." She put her arms around
herself and shivered. "I'm afraid that if I go in there
my heart will surely break."

"Then don't go in." T.J. put an arm around her
shoulders to reassure her. "I'll check the room out
later."

Grateful, Emily smiled up at him. "I didn't mean
to be so sentimental."

"That's okay," T.J. assured her. "You may not
believe it, but I've been known to get sentimental a
time or two myself."

She glanced at up T.J.'s clear blue eyes, which
shone with compassion. "Surely not," she teased.
"Not a strong man like you?"

"Strong in the eye of a generous beholder," T.J.
replied with a wry shrug. "But even a rock can
break."

"Oh no, not you." Emily pointed to the door
across the hall. "That's the only other bedroom. It
was mine."

"Are you game to open the door, or do you want
to consider bunking on the living room couch?"

Emily shuddered. "No way! I used to think the

couch was made of horsehair, or something worse and made to last forever. I remember Aunt Emily used to have to cover it with a soft cotton throw before anyone could sit on it.''

After she opened the door to her bedroom, T.J. wandered around the room, lifting dusty white sheets to check what was underneath. There was a single bed, covered with a handmade patchwork quilt. A doll nestled against a pillow. A young child's maple desk, a matching chair and a bookcase that still contained some of Emily's books were up against the double windows. As if waiting for the room's occupant to return, an unfinished jigsaw puzzle was on the desk.

"Yours?" T.J. leaned over the desk and tried to fit a small section into the puzzle. "Looks as if it's almost complete. Maybe we can finish it tonight."

Emily's hand covered his. "No, please."

"Why not?"

"If we finish the puzzle, everything is over."

T.J. studied the puzzle. It was a picture of the Grand Canal in Venice. "Maybe it's the idea of closing the door on the past that bothers you."

Emily looked over his shoulder. "My aunt gave it to me after I told her how much I wanted to go there. I just feel I have to leave it there. As long as Aunt Emily left it unfinished, I feel as if I can come home again if I want to."

"She probably kept it there to remind her of

you.'' T.J. remarked thoughtfully. ''Looks as if she expected you to come back someday.''

''Maybe,'' Emily agreed. Maybe T.J. was right. Maybe she *did* belong here. She'd already given up her dream of marrying and having a family. But not before she tried to make at least one of her dreams come true.

T.J. took her in his arms. ''Em,'' he murmured, and pushed her hair away from her eyes, ''I'm sure everything will come together for you in the end. Sell the cottage to me. That way no stranger will take over. I've told you, you can come back for a visit anytime you want to.''

He put a finger under her chin, raised her face to his and kissed.

As she drank in his kiss, Emily sensed it was somehow different from the other brief embraces they'd shared and that this time, his heart and soul were in the kiss.

Was the kiss just an attempt to help ease her heartache? If so, it awakened all her senses and sent them soaring. The scent of his shaving lotion, the taste of him, the sound of his low, sensuous voice murmuring words of reassurance turned all the nerve endings in her body on fire. Wanting more of him, she burrowed deeper into the strong arms that held her.

''Em?'' he murmured against her lips. There was

a question in his voice, a yearning that mirrored her own.

She was sensible enough to realize love might not have anything to do with the heart-stopping moment. Still, the strength in the arms that held her and the tenderness in the eyes that gazed at her soothed her very soul.

He'd told her to let him know if she ever wanted or needed him. She not only needed him, she wanted him. And she wanted him now. It was time to forget the past. To stop worrying about what the future might bring. It was time to cherish the present. She smiled up at him.

"You're sure?" he asked, as if he sensed her thoughts.

Emily nodded wordlessly. When he still hesitated, she gave him the answer he was waiting for. "Yes."

Chapter Nine

T.J. gazed down on her with a yearning expression that she sensed matched her own. "You'll never be sorry for trusting me, Em. I promise."

"I know." She leaned away, just far enough to release the top button on his shirt. "I have to confess," she said with a saucy smile as she went back to work and undid the next button, "I seem to have a preoccupation with your chest."

"How about the rest of me?" He asked, his gaze sent heat rushing through her.

"That too, at least the parts of you I can see," she said with a shaky laugh. "I'm afraid it started at the construction site when I saw the sun shining on your bare skin. And kept right when I was bathing you to bring down your fever." Her hands roamed over his chest as she met his eyes.

He captured her hands in both of his and kissed each knuckle, one by one. "You mean you wanted to take advantage of my weakened condition?" He laughed when she blushed. "Too bad I wasn't in any shape to reciprocate, sweetheart, because I had designs on you, too. He pulled back, and, to Emily's surprise, his expression grew serious and more than a little surprised. "Who knows this might actually turn out to be true love."

Emily lowered her head to hide her reaction and moved to the next button. This was the first time the word "love" had been mentioned between them. An impossible dream considering they'd only recently met, and yet...

"My turn," T.J. went on softly. He held her away while he unbuttoned her blouse, drew it over her shoulders and down to her waist. "You aren't the only one with a fantasy, sweetheart. I've wanted to do this for a long time, too."

"It's a good thing this time we're both conscious and wide-awake, isn't it?" she whispered.

"Wide awake and eager," he agreed before he turned her around and kissed the dimples on the back of her shoulders, the sensitive spot on the nape of her neck. His heated fingers burned her skin as he unbuttoned her lacy bra. He hooked his fingers under the slender straps, and they fell off her shoulders. She shivered.

"Cold?" She wrapped her arms around her middle, shook her head and turned into his arms.

"No, just eager."

T.J. ran his hands over her slender torso and

glanced over at the bed. "I have a remedy, but first…"

His voice trailed off as he removed the rest of her clothing. He ran his hands over her sensitive skin. "Em," he murmured softly, "you're every bit as beautiful as I thought you would be."

Afraid to lose the erotic moment, Emily rained kisses on his bare chest. This time it was his turn to shiver.

"Cold?" she parroted. "I have a remedy for that, too."

She drew his shirt off his shoulders and kissed a scar on his chest. She traced the mark with her finger. "How did you get the scar?"

"I'm afraid I'm not the most agile guy around. It's not that I look for trouble, but trouble has a way of finding me," he added with shrug. "Got a few more scars to prove it, too."

"Where?" she asked, glancing over his tanned chest.

"Em, you don't want to know." He shrugged out of his jeans, his boxers and pulled the dust cover from the bed. He drew back the quilt and, with a wicked grin that sent her senses soaring, he carried her over to the bed.

"You're a miracle, Em," he murmured. He dropped to one knee and gazed down at her. "I'm not quite sure just when I realized my admiration for you had changed to desire, but I want to kiss every inch of you.'' He dropped beside her and ran a gentle finger over her navel, around the curve of her hips and up to her breasts until she thought she couldn't take it anymore. ''Everything about you is a miracle.''

''Are you only going to talk about miracles?'' she asked, taking his face between her hands. She dropped little kisses along his chin, his Adam's apple. ''How about creating a new one.''

''Can do.'' To her delight, T.J. gathered her into his arms, swept his hands over her nude back, her waist, her aching breasts, warming her with his kisses until she was almost mindless with longing.

''More,'' she whispered into his lips. He grinned and tongued her breasts until they rose in urgent peaks. His lips traced a path down to her waist, her thighs. His hands followed and caressed each sensitive spot he'd kissed.

When she couldn't bear the ecstasy that threatened to engulf her, she pulled him over her and took him to her.

Streaks of electrical current ran through her as he filled her. Her arms embraced him, her legs held him close. Murmuring tender love words, she met him thrust for thrust, kiss for kiss, until waves of blinding sensations covered her, burst into flames and sent her spiraling into a world she'd never glimpsed before.

She heard him shout her name, felt him shudder as he joined her.

When they finally came back to earth, T.J. gazed down at her with a tender smile. "Warm enough now?"

"Almost," she answered, drifting back to earth. She ran her hands over his back, which was covered with a silken sheen of sweat. Nuzzled his shoulders with little love bites. She held him tight while the flames inside her slowly dimmed. Cuddled in his arms, Emily murmured softly, "I have another confession to make."

"Confess away," he answered. With her still in his arms, he fell to his side and threw a leg over her. "Right now, I'm in the mood to forgive anything. As for doing anything about it, I'm afraid you'll have to give me a few minutes."

"Not that," she laughed, cuddling closer. "It's about something that happened when I first saw the sign advertising the bachelor auction. When I saw you, I felt as if some force drew me in to the auction room."

T.J. fell silent. *When she first saw him on the auction block?* A cold chill ran over his heated body. Was it possible Emily still believed him to be Tim? "Like what?"

"As if we were destined to meet." She laughed. "Crazy, isn't it? Me, in the little town of Placerville, California and you here in Los Angeles. We don't even know the same people or have anything in common.''

''No friends, sure, but as far as having something in common, there's this.'' He kissed the spot between her breasts. ''What else?''

''I knew I'd met you for the first time at the auction. I knew you were the man with me in the photograph. But when I saw you at the construction site, for a few minutes I had the strangest feeling you weren't the same man. You were more handsome and sexier than ever.'' Her hands roamed over his chest as she met his eyes. ''Of course, it was you. How could you be two people?''

T.J. blinked and roused himself from his sexual euphoria. Of all the times for Emily to hint that he might not be the man she'd won at the auction, this was the worst.

Heaven help him, it wasn't the time or the place to confess she'd been right. He wasn't the same man who'd flirted with her from an auction block. He was a man in love with her. He looked down at Emily. She'd fallen asleep in his arms.

To his surprise, he'd found he wanted Emily in all the ways he'd never wanted a woman. He wanted to help her dream of visiting the real Venice come true even if that meant he would have to give up his own dream.

Even after deciding to give Emily a chance to make her childhood dream come true, T.J couldn't sleep. He should have been calm, relaxed, adrift in a sea of contentment after a night of loving Emily. Instead he was wide-awake.

His conscience insisted maybe he'd been wrong in trying to persuade Emily to give up a dream and stay here. He'd meant well. The fact that he'd fallen for her might have clouded his judgment.

He glanced lovingly down at Emily. Curled into his chest, she murmured in her sleep. The first rays of dawn drifting through the curtained window revealed auburn eyelashes resting on porcelain skin. Teardrops lingered at the corner of her eyes.

He wished he could make himself believe her tears were tears of happiness after a night spent in his arms making love. Somehow, he had the uneasy feeling she could just as easily have been lost in a dream of a childhood sheltered by her aunt's loving arms. Arms that had shielded her from the reality of a seriously ill father and a mother too preoccupied with caring for him to give Emily the attention she needed.

To add to his misgivings, his senses told him there was something he needed to do. Now. He wouldn't have taken the message seriously if he hadn't sensed the "something" had to do with Emily.

He stirred restlessly. No way was he going to be able to get any real sleep until he did something about it.

Careful not to awaken Emily, he bent over and

kissed her lightly on her forehead. When she stirred, he murmured soft words of reassurance. Luckily, she fell back to sleep. He cautiously inched his way out of the narrow bed to put on his jeans. Barefoot, so as not to awaken Emily, he padded across the hall and to the door Emily had been reluctant to open when she showed him around the cottage.

The bedroom door opened easily. He groped in the dark until he found the light switch by the door and flipped it on. To his interested gaze, the room was a bedroom like any other bedroom. Covered by a dusty white sheet, a large brass bed filled the center of the room. In a puzzling contrast, he noted that none of the other pieces of furniture had been covered as they had been throughout the house.

A nightstand with an open Bible and a brass letter opener resting on its surface stood beside the double bed. An oak chest of drawers topped with a framed picture of Emily and a bowl of potpourri stood on the other side of the bed. Two landscape paintings that, on closer inspection, were signed by a young Emily, hung on the wall. A yellow oak rocker, a lamp, and a padded footstool completed the furnishings.

T.J. inhaled the lingering scent of lavender potpourri and gazed thoughtfully at the photograph of a youthful Emily. Together with the Bible and the stories she'd told him about her aunt, the Bible and the photograph told him volumes of what had been dear to the heart of the room's late occupant. The realization of their loving relationship sent a warmth through his own heart. And, crazy as it seemed to him, he began to feel a part of that relationship.

The room, its former occupant, and Emily's memories seemed almost to have become his own. They gave him another reason to buy the cottage. Rather than see it sold to someone who might tear it down, he had to restore the cottage to its vintage glory.

That didn't really surprise him. Since he'd met Emily, he'd been on the receiving end of enough unsettling events in his own life to change him from a rational, pragmatic man to a believer in miracles.

What was there about the room that drew him there? Curiosity, or the builder's instinct, told him the strong odor of mildew signaled the room needed attention.

He checked the room again. On the surface, there was still nothing unusual.

Except that one of the lathe-and-plaster walls appeared to have been damaged by water. He remembered smelling mildew when he'd first entered the cottage.

He was a poor example of a builder, he thought as he ran his hand across the damp wall. After he'd noticed a hole in the roof on his first visit to the cottage, any contractor worth his salt would have checked for interior water damage right away. Especially a builder with more than twenty years of experience restoring buildings.

He went to the door and walked across the hall to check on Emily. Reassured she was still asleep, he made his way back to the room to consider just how much work would be involved in repairing the roof and interior walls of the cottage. And yet, as he stood there, he couldn't help wondering why a man in his right mind would be inspecting water damage when a warm and loving woman was waiting for him in the bedroom across the hall.

"T.J.? What in the world are you doing in here?"

A sleepy and disheveled Emily, wearing the shirt he'd left behind, stood in the doorway rubbing her eyes. Open to her waist and ending at pink-tinged thighs, the shirt managed to reveal more than it concealed. To add to his physical and mental discomfiture, the erotic sight sent his mind racing back to the incredible moment last night when Emily had said yes.

Memories of tangled bodies, passionate kisses, and a journey into a memorable erotic experience with a woman he'd begun to think of as his destiny sent his body stirring once again. If he had any sense, he would kiss her lips, her slender neck and her pouting breasts. Take her back to bed and bury himself in her warmth.

"I'm sorry I awakened you, Em," he said with an effort to make sense out of his midnight wandering, "but I couldn't sleep. I just wandered in here so as not to awaken you."

"In the middle of the night?"

"Guess so," he answered sheepishly. "I gotta tell you, I'd much rather be back in bed."

Emily slid her arm through his and rested her head on his shoulder. "And all I can say, Mr. Kirkpatrick, is let's go back to bed. I'm cold."

With a last look around the room, T.J. put his arm around Emily's shoulder and turned her into his arms. "You are cold," he muttered, and nuzzled her neck. "I know just the way to warm you up."

"I can't wait." Emily lifted her face for his kiss. "I can't think of another place I'd rather be than in bed with you." With a lingering glance around the room, she led T.J. back to her bedroom.

"This bed could be a little larger," Emily murmured as she dropped tiny kisses over T.J.'s nude chest. "It doesn't give me much room to explore the rest of you."

For T.J. the bed was the perfect size—the closer she was, the greater the contact. What had gone on before was only a prelude to the present. He intended to take his time and try to show Emily how much she meant to him. "Explore away," he said as he slid her over him. "Now that we're both awake, I intend to do some detailed exploring myself."

Emily smiled into his eyes. "You do have a way

with me, T.J. But, before I go any further, is there some name I can call you? T.J. sounds so imperial.''

He ran his fingers over her lips and watched the colors in her hazel eyes change. Gray and blue were joined by warm streaks of gold and green as her eyes mirrored her thoughts. She was right. Initials were impersonal, a means by which a guy could hide his emotions, something he realized he'd done for most of his life. Maybe it was time to open himself to Emily. ''You can call me Tom.''

''Tom,'' she repeated as she held his face between her hands and nipped at his chin. ''And I really am Em.''

''I guess I've known that all along,'' he replied with a tender kiss. '''Em' suits you.''

''Be careful how you use it,'' she cautioned. ''Only two other people have called me by that name. And one of them is gone.'' By asking him to call her Em, Emily felt as if she'd given him her heart to hold.

T.J. smiled up into her eyes. ''I've got to go soon, so why don't we get back to more explorations?''

His teasing glance sent waves of heat coursing through her. The need to belong to him again was strong. Each kiss she gave him was a renewal of her trust in him. Otherwise she knew she wouldn't have been able to invite him to call her ''Em.''

Emily was still asleep when T.J. quietly dressed and left the cottage. He left a note on her pillow telling her he would see her later, but he had a disturbing feeling there was something he'd left undone.

If anyone needed to talk things over with a mind more rational than his own, it was he. Who else would listen to talk of spirits? And who else would understand why he'd decided to ask Emily to marry him?

"SO YOU SEE, DAD, I'm between a rock and a hard place," T.J. said when he'd finished telling his father about Emily. "After spending the past few days with Emily and realizing what a wonderful woman she is, I'm thinking of asking her to marry me."

His father regarded him under raised eyebrows. "Well, that's certainly a first. I'd almost given up on you."

"It surprised me, too," T.J. answered as he paced the floor. In the living room, a grandfather clock sounded the noon hour. "I suddenly realized Emily had all the attributes I wanted in a woman. She's honest, caring and loving. She treasures the past and admires all the things about it that I do. I realized how much when she showed me the interior of the cottage and told me all about her life there with her aunt."

His father regarded him thoughtfully. "If you've made up your mind, why are you here?"

T.J. paused in his pacing. Embarrassed at the

thought that this would be the first time he had freely discussed his gratitude for having been adopted, he gazed at his father. "You may think I'm nuts, but even though I love Emily, I don't think I have the right to get married now."

"The right to fall in love and get married?" His father's eyebrows arched. "You've got to be kidding!"

"Nope. It may sound weird," T.J. answered, "but it's the truth. I've never told you how I felt about your adopting me and Tim, but here goes." Unaccustomed to sharing his inner thoughts, he took a deep breath. "I've always felt grateful to you and Mom for deciding to adopt Tim and me instead of opting to hold out for infants. I guess my way of showing my gratitude is by helping with Tim and taking over the day-to-day running of the business since your accident." He smiled sheepishly. "It sounds stupid, but I've always thought love and marriage would get in the way of those responsibilities."

His father pulled himself into his wheelchair and nodded. "Come on into the kitchen. After what you've just said, I could use a cup of black coffee." As he wheeled himself into the kitchen, he added, "I've often wondered why you worked harder and played less than most boys of your age. Now that you've come this far, you might as well get everything off your chest. Anything else on your mind?"

"Some," T.J. answered, relieved by his admission. "But first, I'm going to make us a pot of blacker-than-sin coffee. You can supervise."

"Lead on." His father laughed. "You don't need my advice about making coffee, but it's beginning to sound as if we're both going to need it."

T.J. led the way into the kitchen where his late mother's loving touches were everywhere—in the cheery green curtains, the "apple" pattern of the dishes in the open shelves and in the copper plates hung around the walls. A handwoven rag rug rested under a maple breakfast set. He relaxed, sure in the conviction his mother would have loved Emily.

Under his father's thoughtful gaze, he rummaged in the pantry for a can of coffee, filled the coffeemaker with water and set it to drip. When the smell of fresh coffee filled the air, he filled two cups and settled down at the kitchen table.

"I've never told you this before," he began, "but I think it's time to say it now."

"Shoot." His father sipped the hot coffee. "I'm all ears."

"I never talked about it, but I've never forgotten the day my birth mother left me and Tim at the foundation. I used to think something had to be wrong with us, with me. Bottom line, I never really felt worthy of being anyone's son."

"Stop right there," his father said. He locked his

gaze with T.J. "You and Tim are the best sons a man could ask for, and don't you forget it!"

"Thanks, Dad." T.J. gazed into his coffee cup. If he didn't, he knew he'd break up. "Anyway, I worked extra hard to make you glad you adopted us. And that's not the whole of it," he said when his father started to protest again. "I made up my mind that when I did find the right woman, she would have to be the kind of woman who would never walk away from me or any children we might have."

"That's a heavy burden for a man to carry," his father said. He toyed with his coffee cup, then met T.J.'s eyes. "If I'd known, I would have told you long ago that when we saw the protective way you held your little brother's hand and refused to leave him, we were hooked." He paused and cleared his throat. "Maybe your mother and I didn't try hard enough to show you how much we loved you, but we did and I still do. I respect you as a grown man, too. But let's face it, you *are* a grown man now. It's time you buried the past."

T.J. grimaced and stared at his empty coffee cup. "Easier said than done."

"Of course it's not easy." Thornton Kirkpatrick heaved a sigh and sat back in his wheelchair. "I've been there, done that myself. And paid the price. As long as we're talking man to man, I might as well tell you that as a young man, I was a lot like Tim, dead set on enjoying myself and not answering to anyone but myself.''

T.J. shook his head in disbelief. This wasn't the father he knew and loved. ''Not you, Dad. You've set an example I've tried to live by.''

''Maybe so,'' his father answered wryly, ''but by the time I faced up to loving Lorena, to my lasting regret, I'd already had a vasectomy. That's why we opted for adoption. Considering our ages, we couldn't take an infant, anyway. We thanked our lucky stars for the opportunity to adopt you and your brother. So, don't fool yourself. You don't owe me anything. If you love Emily, go for it.''

T.J. swallowed the lump in his throat. He reached for his father's hand and squeezed it hard. It couldn't have been easy for his father to confess why he couldn't have natural children. Or that, knowing he'd had a vasectomy, he'd ultimately betrayed the woman he loved.

If his father had the courage to admit his failings, it was time for T.J. to take a hard look at his own. ''Emily has plans to move on, and I want to be with her. It's a hell of a conflict.''

''Tell her so. Emily needs to have a loving anchor as much as you do, son. Dreams are like carrots on a stick. We might need them to keep us going, but that doesn't mean the carrot is our ultimate goal.''

T.J. continued to pace the room. His father's observations about Emily were almost the same as his own. There had to be something more to Emily's dreams than a trip to Italy. Maybe she only spoke of that one dream because the present had held little promise of any other dream coming true.

"Maybe you're right, Dad. I'll think about it. At any rate, now that I know why Daniels lied to Emily about her inheritance, I intend to keep an eye on her interests. And when the time comes when she inherits, I'm going to buy the property and give it to her for a wedding present."

"That's more like it. Maybe it hasn't occurred to you," his father added with a wry smile, "but I could use a grandchild or two."

T.J. stopped in his pacing. He'd almost gotten used to the idea of seeing Emily as his wife. And had even thought of their children. What kind of father would he make?

"Kind of early to think of grandchildren, isn't it, Dad?"

"At my age," his father said, and grinned, "it's never too soon. But kids aside, it's time for you to take up your own identity. Stop trying to be T. J. Kirkpatrick Historical Building Restoration all by yourself. Take my advice, Tom, and get yourself a life. But before you do, I strongly suggest you tell Emily the same story you've just told me. I think it just might clear up the trust problem."

T.J. saw the gray lines around his father's lips, his tired eyes, the dark brown hair that was rapidly turning gray. He was ready to kick himself. He'd been so immersed in his own problems that he hadn't realized his father had any regrets of his own. No wonder he wanted the love and affection of grandchildren to fill his life.

His father was right. It was time to become Thomas Jefferson Kirkpatrick and Family instead of T. J. Kirkpatrick, restorer of vintage buildings.

Now, all he had to do was to convince Emily. He loved her.

Chapter Ten

When T.J. discovered the end of the summer season brought with it an annual carnival in the beach city of Venice, he made plans to be there. For the seventh time, he found himself with his hand on the phone. He ached to call Emily and tell her he wanted to pick up where he'd left off. To tell her he loved her and wanted to be her husband.

Then he remembered. She had no phone. And even if she did, after he'd left her with just a note on her pillow, he wasn't sure she'd be too happy to hear from him. Maybe it would be better to surprise her, catch her unaware. To show her a side of himself he'd foolishly refused to recognize until now. He'd shouldered more responsibilities than he had to. To show her he was an ordinary man with the wants and needs of an ordinary man.

Emily was the woman he needed and wanted.

His father's words of advice came back to him.

If he truly loved Emily, and he was sure he did, it was time to tell her so.

He studied the colorful carnival brochure he'd found in a Venice supermarket. He needed a costume. His first thought was of the Straw Man of *Wizard of Oz* fame, a popular character that had always been one of his favorites. Still considering the mood he was in, it was a perfect fit. After the way he'd mishandled his relationship with Emily, he had to convince Emily he loved her. How could he have been so stupid to ask her to trust him and then leave her with a note on her pillow instead of kissing her awake and saying goodbye the way lovers do?

He remembered the vintage cardboard movie posters he and Emily had admired earlier at the Beaumont Hotel. Unless he was mistaken, she was sure to remember his rueful remark about relating to the Straw Man when he'd been an awkward kid. With a sharp mind like hers, she was bound to recall the remark in a blink of an eye. He had to come up with another idea to surprise her.

"Hi, bro!"

At the sound of Tim's voice, the reminder that he'd virtually been roped into meeting Emily flashed into T.J.'s mind. He swung around to confront his brother, the last person he wanted to see right now. "What are you doing here?"

Tim blinked and looked his surprise. "I work here, remember?"

T.J. struggled to rein in his frustration. Tim was a working partner in the family business. Instead of being annoyed, he should have been grateful Tim was ready to go to work. It was just damned inconvenient to have him turn up now.

Gazing at his grinning brother, T.J. had a sinking premonition Tim's return boded no good. If Emily caught a glimpse of them together, she'd have to know the truth. And hate herself for not believing him when he'd tried to tell her the truth. He couldn't afford to take a chance.

"I thought you were away on business," he growled. "Monkey business, more likely. As if you haven't already caused enough problems around here."

Tim grinned. "You're not going to hold that bachelor auction caper against me, are you?"

"I'm not sure," T.J. replied. "Would it do any good?" Wary of what his brother might come up with next, he wasn't going to give away the status of his relationship with Emily.

"Nah," an obviously unrepentant Tim replied. "I figured I was doing you a favor by sending her here. Not that the lady in question wasn't mighty attractive. Clever too, or she wouldn't have been able to come up with that temporary marriage-of-convenience scenario."

"If you thought she was so great, little brother, why did you send her to me?"

"Because there was something about her that told me she wasn't the temporary kind," Tim answered cheerfully. "You know me, I make it my business to stay out of the way of serious women. It's different with you, bro. In my book, you're more of a forever kind of guy."

Undecided whether to thank or chew out his brother, T.J. silently stared at him. For a seemingly devil-may-care type of guy, Tim was more astute than he'd given him credit for. Not that he needed Tim to remind him he was the forever kind of man. He just hadn't found a woman he could trust to stick around forever with until now.

His silence seemed to draw Tim's attention in a way T.J. hadn't intended. He braced himself for what was coming next.

"What's the matter, didn't you and the lucky lady hit it off?"

"Maybe." T.J. stuck the Carnival in Venice brochure into a back pocket of his jeans. The last thing he wanted was for Tim to pick up on the carnival.

Or, heaven help him, show up. His rapport with Emily was too new, too tenuous, to risk having Tim show up before he'd set the stage for the truth. First, he had to make sure he had a solid relationship with Emily.

"Maybe?" Tim echoed dubiously. "That's almost as good as saying you don't know. Either you hit it off or you didn't. Want to try again?"

The sound of a skip loader dropping broken bricks and old lumber into a Dumpster cut off T.J.'s reply. Grateful at the interruption, he shuddered when he thought of what Tim might come up with next. More jokes at his expense?

He waited until the strident sounds of the cleanup dimmed. He'd completed his part of the exterior reconstruction. With Tim back as the designated architect-in-charge of rebuilding the interior of the gutted station, now was his own chance to take a few days off.

"Why don't you forget me and Emily and think of getting back to work?" he suggested casually. "I'm sure you have better things to keep you busy than worrying about the two of us."

"Emily?" Tim's eyes lit up. "Maybe I was too hasty in setting you up with her. What's she like?"

Perfection, T.J. was tempted to answer. Expressive hazel eyes. An intelligent woman with a heart. A real woman with heated blood in her veins. "Just a woman," he answered, shrugging away any hint of the way he felt about Emily.

Tim's calculating look made T.J. want to kick himself. He should have kept his mouth shut, handed Tim the bundle of blueprints and taken himself out of sight.

Tim eyed him thoughtfully. "If you're on a first-name basis with the lady, things must not have turned out so badly after all. I did you a favor. If you're going to keep her for yourself, you owe me big time."

Favor? Tim's wicked grin made T.J.'s insides clench. To his growing annoyance, Tim actually looked proud of himself. The "favor" had turned T.J.'s ordered life upside down and inside out and he'd wound up falling in love with Emily.

Even his waking and sleeping moments were spent thinking about Emily. And now that he'd made up his mind to win her, he had to try to find a way to keep her in his arms.

He wondered what his chances were of keeping Tim out of sight. "I'll let you know later if it was a favor," he told his brother. He took off his leather tool belt and packed it into his pickup truck. "Right now it may be a toss-up."

"Anything I can do to help?"

Tim looked so falsely contrite that T.J. had to bite back a laugh. "No thanks, I can handle it. You've done enough."

T.J.'s obvious reluctance to tell all must have finally registered with his brother. "That bad, eh?"

"Don't worry," T.J. hurriedly assured his brother. "I'm working on a plan."

"She didn't notice there was a difference between us, did she? Honest, I wouldn't have sent her over here if everyone hasn't said we look enough alike to be twins."

More frustrated about his chances with Emily

than he was willing to admit, T.J. ran his fingers through his hair. "For what it's worth, I tried to tell Emily we were look-alike brothers—with zip results. I have to find a way to make her accept the truth without upsetting her."

"You're just the man to do it," Tim said confidently. "Hang in there."

"Yeah, by the tips of my fingernails," T.J. muttered as he headed for Duke with Tim in tow. "Do me a favor and stay out of sight. The last thing I need is for Emily to catch a glimpse of us together before I've set the stage."

NO CLOSER TO REALIZING her dream of seeing Italy than she'd been at the time Daniels had disappeared, his continued absence began to worry Emily. Either the shyster lawyer was waiting for things to cool down, or he was working on another way to cheat her out of her inheritance.

To add to her frustration, she hadn't heard from T.J. since two nights before when he'd made love to her. The note he'd left behind two days ago hadn't been enough to convince her he wasn't another Sean.

She still missed him. Missed his confidence, his strength. The way he'd seemed to believe in her instead of dismissing her as a dreamer. And, most of all, she thought, as she listened to her lonely heart, she missed the wonderful way he'd made her feel in his arms.

She glanced at the colorful Carnival in Venice brochure she'd picked up at the nearby convenience store where she'd gone shopping for groceries. She'd been so mired in missing T.J. she'd almost forgotten the annual celebration.

She searched in her dresser for her favorite costume. With a few alternations at the bustline and at the hem, it appeared to be in good shape.

If this was going to be the last carnival she would attend, she was going to enjoy it.

SQUINTING IN THE BRIGHT SUN, Emily stood on the cottage porch and inhaled the familiar sweet scent of honeysuckle vines. Pleased at the reminder of her childhood, she lifted her face into the fresh ocean breeze flowing across the canal. The day was perfect, the sun was shining, and there wasn't a cloud in the sky. Even the blue morning glories that grew on the fence separating the cottage from the newly built modern condominium complex next door looked brighter than usual. The only thing that marred the afternoon was the thought that if she sold the cottage, another concrete condominium complex would take its place.

She sighed and glanced at the wooden swing in which she'd spent so many happy hours. The paned windows, the green shutters, and the honeysuckle vines where bees vied for honey.

It was no use living in the past, she told herself. With her future still up in the air, at least she could treasure the present.

She turned her gaze on the bustling activity in front of her. Booths selling items imported from Italy had been assembled and looked ready for business. Colorful balloons were being taped to the ornate concrete bridges that crossed the canal. Clusters of small bands were playing, sidewalk musicians were strolling through the growing crowd. The mouthwatering scent of freshly popped popcorn and the cotton candy she had loved as a child tickled her nose.

"Emily? Emily Holmes, is that you?" Fiona Ridley, a one-time neighbor of her aunt's called to her from the sidewalk. Like the fictional Mary Poppins, she wore a dated cotton dress, a straw hat, and carried an umbrella to shield her from the strong sun. "I'm so happy to see you again, my dear," she said as she bustled up the walk. "I just can't wait to find out if the rumors are true!"

"What rumors, Mrs. Ridley?" Emily smiled her welcome. She knew from experience Mrs. Ridley was a one-woman telegraph line with a heart bigger than the rumors she spread.

"I heard your aunt's cottage was going to be sold, dear. Is that true?"

"I'm not sure." Emily glanced over at the condominium complex that she'd heard had been built after Mrs. Ridley's cottage had fallen to a wrecking ball. A chill passed over her at the thought her late aunt's home might suffer a similar fate. "The decision isn't mine to make. Aunt Emily's estate hasn't been settled yet."

As if she wanted to make sure they were alone, her companion glanced around her. "I think I should tell you I've noticed strange men wandering around the cottage lately. There was one man in particular—a tall, handsome gentleman. Handsome enough to turn a woman's head," she tittered before she caught herself. "Gracious sakes, but the man was full of questions!"

Emily's thoughts swung to lawyer Daniels. "What did you tell him?"

"Nothing, my dear, not a thing," Mrs. Ridley assured her. "As you must know, I mind my own business. But, since I live in one of those condominiums next door now, I can't help noticing things." She blushed. "I thought I'd better warn you. The man could be up to no good."

Emily nodded politely. Who else besides Tom and the lawyer knew she'd moved into the cottage?

Sean? He didn't even know where Emily had gone. He was certainly handsome and charming on the surface, but self-centered and untrustworthy underneath. She'd learned that the hard way.

T.J.? Surely he had no reason to skulk around the cottage. He'd offered to buy and restore the cottage; she was on the verge of agreeing.

Daniels, on the other hand, may have gone out of town on business, but he could have sent someone to check up on her. In spite of what T.J. had confidently said, she was sure the man wouldn't take her moving into the cottage lightly before the estate was settled.

That's all she needed. An ex-fiancé, a shady lawyer, and a man she'd grown to love but who couldn't seem to make up his mind about her. He'd asked her to trust him, now alone and in broad daylight, she wasn't so sure if she could.

She remembered sensing a strange presence outside the cottage early this morning. When she'd gotten up the courage to look, no one was there. She'd chalked it up to an overactive imagination, but she'd have to be more careful now.

"Thank you, Mrs. Ridley," she answered politely. "I'll be sure to keep an eye out for strangers."

"That's good, dear," Mrs. Ridley replied. "And do enjoy yourself at the carnival today. It's a pity your aunt isn't here to enjoy it with you."

Emily smiled and picked up her plush toy dog and went to join the revelers.

By dusk, costumed revelers thronged the path that ran alongside the canal. Booths selling Italian sausage rolls and other delicacies had lines of hungry diners. Strolling musicians were playing nostalgic Italian love songs. Sounds of laughter filled the air.

"Gondola ride, signora?"

Emily shook her head. Gondola rides, she mused wistfully as she wandered along the thronged path, were for lovers, not for someone like her. After her recent experience with Sean, and with T.J.'s continued absence, she doubted she would ever qualify as any man's love.

A costumed pirate, his face partially obscured with a black silk mask across his eyes caught her attention. Clad in a striking black velvet costume, knee-high black leather boots, his presence was powerfully male. A wide, black hat with a golden plume waving in the breeze covered his bandana-covered hair. At first glance, she'd admired his costume, but now she had the vague notion he was following her. Uneasy, she looked away.

Her attention diverted, she stumbled on a large wide crack in the sidewalk and dropped the tube of cotton candy. Before she could regain her footing, a masked French gendarme stepped in front of her and caught her arm. His teeth flashed in a wide smile below his black mask, but she shivered as she sensed there was no smile in his eyes.

"You have a problem, mademoiselle? May I be of service?"

"No, thank you, I'm really fine. Just shaken up a

bit.'' Startled by the unexpectedly firm grip on her arm, Emily tried to pull away. His grasp tightened and he pulled her toward the canal. ''Perhaps a gondola ride?''

She looked for help and tried to twist away. ''Let me go!''

The pirate materialized at her side. ''Apparently, the lady isn't interested,'' he said smoothly, his hand on his sword. ''I suggest you let her go.''

Emily's heart skipped. The pirate's low voice sounded familiar, but she couldn't be sure it really was T.J. What she did know was that, whoever he was, the sword at his side was real and he sounded as if he meant business.

This was supposed to be a harmless costume carnival, she thought wildly as she looked around for help. There were more policemen in sight, but, heaven help her, she couldn't tell if they were real or the carnival variety.

The gendarme reluctantly released her arm. ''Apparently, I was mistaken, mademoiselle. My apologies.'' With a cold glance at the pirate, he bowed and lost himself in the crowd.

''Who *are* you?'' Emily demanded when she and the pirate were left standing in a sea of carnival celebrants. Someone blew a horn in her ear and showered her with confetti. She stumbled again. He steadied her against his chest for a moment then let her go. "Later." Before she could thank him, he disappeared into the crowd.

The brief encounter was enough for Emily. She'd know T.J.'s embrace anywhere. After all, he was the man who'd made love to her. A man who had stolen her heart. The faint word "later" echoed in the salty night air.

She was sure he'd come back, but she was still troubled. After the way he'd left, should she want him to?

Although the night was warm and flaming torches lit the dark blue sky, she shivered in her white voile blouse and checkered blue pinafore.

Her uneasy feeling that something beyond her control was going on brought shivers to her skin long after she started back home. She reached the cottage porch and stopped when she sensed a presence.

"T.J.? Tom? Is that you?"

The velvet-clad pirate moved to her side and removed his mask. "Yes."

She was relieved. Angry with him or not, what woman could have resisted a man who had saved her from some unknown harm and who continued to stir her senses?

"Why didn't you tell me who you were when I asked you before?"

"Sorry, I was waiting for the right time and the right place," he answered, and moved closer. "I wanted a more private setting—there's so much I want to tell you.''

Emily backed away from his outstretched arms and shook her head. ''I wanted to talk to you, too.''

''Go ahead,'' he agreed, eyeing her the way a cat surveys his prey. If he kept looking at her like that, she'd be lost before she had a chance to tell him how she felt about his leaving her with only a note.

She drew a shaky breath, conscious of his warm presence beside her. ''I'm tired of waiting for the men in my life to make up their minds about wanting me. First there was Sean, and now you. How could you have left me with only a note after you made love to me and asked me to trust you? Why didn't you awaken me? Or call?''

He could see the hurt in her eyes and, before the night was through, he intended to kiss the hurt away. He threw his hat, mask and his gloves on the swing. ''I'm sorry. The truth is I had to get away long enough to get my act together.''

''Your act? Let me tell you, your story had better be good. I've had enough of you trying to make up your mind whether or not you care about me.''

To T.J.'s dismay, Emily sounded more upset than before.

''I don't know how good it's going to sound,'' he said with a tentative smile, ''but it's a long story.''

''Then you'd better get started.'' She looked at her watch. ''I'll give you ten minutes.''

T.J. knew he'd hurt Emily, but he'd promised himself to tell her enough of the truth so she could understand him. He'd leave Tim out of his confession for now. If she turned him down, God forbid, at least his conscience, if not his heart, would be eased.

"My story started when I was nine, and I was adopted from the foundation. The same foundation that held the bachelor auction." Emily nodded. "I felt so grateful, I tried to show my gratitude. When I was old enough, I took on responsibilities that left me hardly any time to be a real kid. Although I realize it was my choice, I know I didn't have to do that."

Emily could tell from his eyes that he found it difficult to admit to his background. As for trying to pay his parents back by not living his own life, that was another story. "I'm sure you've tried to do the right thing, but I don't see what your being adopted has to do with me."

"Just this. As a kid, I thought I was left at the Foundation for Homeless Children like a package to be reclaimed later. I even decided early on that I would never get married, have children and have it happen to them. And if I did get married, it would be to a woman who would stick by me and with any children we might have."

Emily's heart began to pound. Was he trying to

tell her he didn't love her? "And you've never found the right woman?"

He reached for her. She backed away. She wanted the whole truth.

"Not until I met you. And then, stupid me, I got to worrying about that dream of yours, which would take you out of here. I thought it was a choice between the dream or me. I convinced myself you could do both."

"You never asked me, or let me make the choice," she answered with wounded eyes. "Trust is a two-way street. Does that mean making love to me was merely an impulse?"

He wanted to take her in his arms and show her how much he did care for her. The hurt look in her eyes warned him it was touch-and-go. "Of course not. I've never been one to give in to impulse. The other night was no impulse. I wanted to make you see we belonged together. I wanted to convince you your dream could be fulfilled right here."

She blushed. "I remember a few times when you gave in to an impulse."

At the reminder of passionate love scenes, it was his turn to flush. "I remember a couple of impulsive embraces, too, but they were nothing like that night."

"You still haven't told me why you're here now."

"I decided it was time to be up-front with you.

I love you, Em." He waited until he saw her eyes clear, the frown on her forehead disappear. "So what would you say if I asked you to marry me?"

"I'd say I have some things to think over. Some omissions can be forgiven, but breaking my heart over you isn't one."

T.J. felt a despair creep over him. If he lost Emily now... "You're sure? I never wanted to break your heart."

"I'm sure," she echoed. "I do love you, but you keep waxing hot and cold. I've been down that road before, and I can't do it again. I'm not sure I can trust you enough to marry you."

T.J. gazed at the determined look in her eyes, her set lips.

His heart sank. Emily was right. Without trust, there could be love, but without it, there couldn't be marriage.

Chapter Eleven

Emily locked the door behind T.J. with a heavy heart. Her head was pounding with the beginning of a giant headache, and from its intensity, she knew the pain wasn't likely to go away anytime soon.

Too disturbed to even try to sleep, she curled up on the window seat and watched the carnival celebration wind down for the night.

Maybe T.J. had been right. Maybe she *had* been fooling herself. Maybe the Venice outside her window *was* the Venice of her dreams.

Now that she was living in the cottage, she began to suspect the dream of going to Italy might have been an attempt to recapture the happier days of her childhood.

She recalled telling T.J. sometimes a person can't go home again. Tonight, with her childhood memories drifting back to her, she felt as though she'd never left.

She rested her chin on her knees and faced the

truth. She wasn't the young girl who spent her summers with her aunt. The dream closest to her heart wasn't visiting Italy. She was a grown woman whose real dream was to recreate the loving home her Aunt Emily had made for her each summer.

Given the opportunity, she would have created that dream with a strong and loving man.

T.J. could have been that man.

No sooner than she'd asked him to leave, she'd been tempted to hurl herself into his arms and ask him not to go. She'd yearned to taste his lips one more time, to feel his strong arms around her taking her to the magical world only he had been able to create.

Her heart had urged her to call him back; her pride hadn't allowed her to.

Her heart ached with still-vivid memories. Of the way he had rained kisses over her skin when he'd taken her in his arms and made them one. Of his warm, blue eyes gazing down on her while he made passionate love to her. Of the way she'd given him her heart and her soul.

Could she have been so in love with love she hadn't taken time to realize T.J. had held part of himself back?

She closed the velvet drapes, checked the windows to make sure they were securely fastened before she headed for her bedroom. It was time to decide on the direction her life would have to take.

Letting go of a precious childhood dream was hard enough. The possibility of losing T.J. in the bargain was even worse.

To add to her uncertainty, she tried to imagine what her aunt would think of T.J.

She hesitated at the door to her aunt's bedroom. Even with T.J. beside her, she hadn't been able to bring herself to go inside because of her childhood memories, so how could she go in now without breaking her heart over those same memories?

She turned away and went into her own room. The rose curtains, the quilt on the bed and the matching throw pillows on the bed had all been made by her Aunt Emily to make a lonely little girl feel at home. She glanced around the room and sensed her aunt's presence.

She sank down on the edge of the bed. How in the world could she even have thought to sell the cottage? Or see it torn down to make way for another cold, impersonal condominium complex like the one next door?

And why in the world, she wondered, had she turned away the only man who appeared to empathize with her when she told him about her happy memories of visiting here every summer?

She changed into a nightgown, curled up on top of the quilt and cradled a pillow where T.J.'s masculine scent lingered. She thought of the moments when his hands had stroked her heated body, of his strong, demanding lips on hers. And of the friction created by heated skin sliding over heated skin. She finally fell into a twilight sleep where images of T.J. continued to haunt her.

A sound from the other room awakened her.

She put on a robe, crossed the hall and opened the door to her aunt's bedroom. The strong scent of her aunt's lavender potpourri filled the air.

"I'm home, Aunt Emily," she whispered, knowing in her heart of hearts she belonged here."

There was no answer, but she really hadn't expected one.

Emily smiled as she remembered her beloved aunt rocking gently back and forth with a young Emily in her lap. Reading from her favorite story about shoes and ships and sealing wax, of cabbages and kings. And of the wise Duchess who'd said there was a moral behind everything. Tonight, instead of a moral there seemed to be a message. She was home again.

The bedroom looked to be the same as when T.J. had mentioned the mildewed wall and had started to investigate the source.

She blushed to remember that night—the night she'd told him to forget the wall. To come back to bed and keep her warm. And the magical moments that had followed.

A gust of salty air blew through the open window. In the stillness of the night, she could hear the sound of the pounding ocean surf a block away. Under the billowing lace curtains, a vinyl window shade clapped against the window frame.

Relieved that the rattle of the shade's wooden weight was the sound that had awakened her, Emily closed the window and drew the curtains closed. And yet, something about the room continued to nag at her.

Emily gazed uneasily at the rocking chair that the gust of wind had set into motion. If she hadn't opened it, who had? Was T.J. right? It wasn't safe for her to be here alone. She turned back to survey the room and the damaged wall where the damp had begun to crumble it.

It was time to forget her pride and call T.J. But she intended to make it clear that she hadn't forgotten the reason she'd sent him away. After her experience with Sean, she didn't intend to be twice a fool.

"HI, SWEETHEART!"

"Don't sweetheart me," Emily tried to ignore the warmth that swept her at the sight of his jeans and a glimpse of a ribbed V-neck T-shirt under his open button-front knit shirt. A T-shirt whose neckline was low enough for her to catch a glimpse of tanned skin she'd so lovingly kissed such a short time ago.

How was she going to have an intelligent conversation with the man when he looked as if he'd walked out of her heart?

She led T.J. into the kitchen where she had a fresh pot of coffee waiting.

She had a firm grip on reality, she told herself, and he wasn't going to sway her with his killer smile and soft words. She poured the coffee and started to tell him about the mildew and the open window.

T.J. interrupted her. "Stop right there, Em. I don't care why you asked me back here, all I need to know is that you did. But I'm telling you that this time I'm not going to leave without our coming to an understanding." He motioned away the cup of coffee.

"I know you think I was taking advantage of you, but the truth is I love you. Not for just today, but wherever you go and whatever happens to us. You're Em, and you always will be. No matter what happens next."

She slid the cup back to him. "That's not why I called, and please don't call me Em. I called because I thought I heard something last night after you left. When I looked around I found a window open in my aunt's room."

T.J. shot out of his chair. "Are you okay? Did they take anything?"

"No, to both questions. But that's not the only reason." She took a deep breath and settled into a chair across from him. "I wanted to apologize for some of the things I said to you."

T.J. should have felt vindicated, but he didn't like the doubt he still heard in her voice. Damn! If he loved Emily and wanted to be her husband, he should have told her so before he left. And not in a note, either.

But trying to make Emily realize the days of him changing his mind were over wasn't the important thing right now. If someone had opened the bedroom window, Emily might be in some kind of danger. "Forget it. After waxing hot and cold, I had it coming." He motioned away cream and sugar. "Just tell me how I can help you."

"I noticed the condition of the bedroom wall and decided it was time to do something about it before the roof caves in."

T.J. drained his coffee cup. "Does that mean you intend to keep the cottage?"

"I think so."

"Thank God," he muttered. "I'd hate to see someone buy it, knock it down and build a cement monstrosity. But before I take a look, I'd like to ask a favor."

Emily gazed at him over the edge of her coffee cup. Her expressive eyes revealed the debate going on in her mind. Should she give him another chance?

"What did you have in mind?"

"All I'm asking for is a chance to explain why I've acted the way I have." He gazed at her with all the tenderness he felt inside him. After he explained, maybe he stood a chance of reaching her.

"Just this," he began slowly. "I want to make you understand how hard it was for me to talk about my hang-ups. I was all mixed up, until I met you." He grinned sheepishly. "There were thoughts I never even admitted to myself until two days ago, let alone to anyone else." He went on to explain his need to prove he could be a good son to his adoptive parents. And his determination not to fall in love and marry a woman who one day might leave him.

She sipped at her coffee and silently gazed back at him. There were dark shadows under her eyes. A frown creased her forehead.

He wasn't home yet.

"I don't know what that had to do with your trusting me," Emily finally answered. "If you had, you would have known what kind of woman I am. I've never walked away from anything or anyone I loved."

"I was wrong to even think so," he agreed, and reached for her hand. "But it seems I had to let go of the past in order to realize how wrong I was. I hope it's not too late."

"I'm not sure," Emily answered, willing herself not to go into his arms. Not yet. Broken hearts didn't mend that easily. "I asked you here to help me find out why the window was open. And to take another look at the bedroom wall.''

Frustrated, T.J. rubbed the back of his neck. He still had to find a way to make her believe in him. To make her realize he had to put aside his own memories before he asked her to marry him. He had to make her believe it was time to create a future together.

"Will you let the window and the wall wait for a little while?" he finally asked. "I'd like to settle whatever has come between us.''

Emily blinked, but he could tell from the way her beautiful eyes warmed she wasn't that angry anymore. He came around the table and drew her into his arms.

"I had to let go of the past in order to make a future for us, Em. Will you?"

She hesitated. "So did I. When I'm in your arms, heaven help me, I can't think of anything else but you," she said with a tumultuous smile.

He captured her lips in his. "Heaven already has helped us both, or we wouldn't be here now," he whispered.

The last of Emily's reservations began to fade in T.J.'s embrace. At first his kiss was tender, then his lips were hard as he delved between hers. The taste of him, the strength of him as he held her to him made her heart sing, her legs weaken and her body warm. She shivered at the intimate way he kneaded her shoulders, tenderly tongued the hollow between her breasts. The rush of desire she'd felt for him the other night was nothing compared to the way she wanted him now.

If he'd been indecisive about wanting her before, surely it had to be different now. Today, she was as sure of his true love as she was sure of how much she loved him.

This was more than mere desire, she told herself as she gave herself up to T.J. This was the true love she'd dreamed of finding. The love she'd been waiting for.

"Will you marry me, Em?"

Emily was silent.

T.J. laughed, picked her up in his arms and carried her to her bed. "You're not going to get away from me, this time, sweetheart. There's nothing to keep us apart now."

Nothing, Emily's heart told her as she plunged into another miracle.

Caution would have to wait, her hungry senses told her. She watched him disrobe. First, the knit shirt came off, then the ribbed T-shirt. The muscles on his tanned arms and chest rippled with his every movement. How could she have forgotten how much she loved him?

"Your turn." He grinned. "On second thought," he said, "maybe it's still my turn."

Mesmerized by the sensuous promise in his voice

and in his clear blue eyes, Emily nodded. She was thrilled by the kisses he dropped on her heated skin as he helped her off with her cotton camp shirt and linen shorts. ''We were made for each other, Em,'' she heard him whisper. She wanted to believe him.

Belonging to him was the most glorious moment in her life. Cuddled in T.J.'s arms, she finally fell asleep.

Sometime later a voice awakened her. ''Em?''

''Um?''

''I'm hungry,'' he said, dropping little kisses along her bare shoulder. ''In fact, I'm starved.''

She smothered a sound of pleasure and turned around to face him. ''If you have more loving in mind, give me a moment to wake up so I can enjoy it.''

''Later,'' he said with a rueful laugh. ''Right now I'm afraid it's the truth. I really am starved.''

''How can you still be hungry after this?'' She waved at the rumpled sheets, the pillows tossed helter-skelter and the tangle of clothing on the floor.

''You may be right,'' he answered with a rueful smile, ''but the truth is, I didn't even stop to eat when you called. As for more of this,'' he tenderly kissed each breast. ''I promise there's going to be a later.''

The doubt that lingered in the back of her mind lifted with each kiss. ''Promises, promises.''

''I never make a promise I don't keep.'' He nuzzled the sensitive skin between her breasts and ran his hands over her shoulders. "I'm still hungry."

"I'll feed you, Mr. Kirkpatrick," she said breathlessly, "but first things first."

"Second things, or maybe third," he teased. "If I'm not mistaken, we've already taken care of the first."

Emily blushed. She *had* invited him here for a reason other than making love with him, but the love shining from his sparkling blue eyes had sidetracked her. If she didn't let him go long enough to check out the window and the wall in her aunt's room, they'd be back to the first item on the list. Even as her body ached for him, reason told her there was a time and place for everything.

"How about checking out the other bedroom while I make some sandwiches?"

"You're a good woman." T.J. stepped into his crumpled jeans and winked as he pulled up his zipper. "Make it a double sandwich, or maybe a triple. All this hard work makes a guy hungry."

Emily blushed at the reminder they'd just spent hours exploring each other. And that one discovery had led to another until they'd lost track of time. "I'll do my part," she said as she headed for the kitchen. "You just make sure you do yours."

Armed with the crowbar he'd brought with him when Emily had called, T.J. made his way across the hall. The sight of the damp, crumbling wall made him grimace. Whatever was wrong with the wall, or with the roof for that matter, it was clearly a major job for T. J. Kirkpatrick Historic Building Restoration. There was little he could do now.

Instead of going back and telling Emily, his curiosity got the better of him. He returned to the room to take a good look. He had to wait while Emily rustled up some sandwiches, anyway.

As for the open window, the blast of ocean air and the clattering window shade that had awakened Emily was easy enough to explain. Someone had obviously left the window open. On the other hand, he remembered with a frown, Emily had told him the cottage hadn't been inhabited for almost five years. Had Daniels or his henchmen gotten inside the cottage?

Until he'd met Emily and visited the cottage, he'd always considered himself a pragmatic man. He was still sensible, but things had changed. In order to keep Emily safe, he had to be detective as well as a restorer of other people's dreams.

His mind awhirl, T.J. started in on the wall. How safe was Emily, living alone in the cottage in its present condition? He wondered. The answer was clear. She wasn't safe. And not because of a hole in the cottage roof or a mildewed wall. But because the cottage's window frames were made of weathered wood with glass panes that could be easily broken into, as someone already had. If not Daniels, then by some homeless drifter.

Either he had to persuade Emily to move in with him until Daniels came back and the estate was settled, or he had to move in with her. Both ideas appealed to him, but the question was, would they appeal to Emily? And what did he have to do to convince her they belonged together?

At what seemed to be an eternity later, he'd chipped away enough of the damaged wall to be able to see behind it. Enthralled, he saw a vintage movie poster advertising an early Greta Garbo movie, *Mata Hari*, set in between the lathe-and-plaster framework. It resembled posters he'd seen on display at museums and auction houses that were carefully encased in protective covering. Never, in the furthest reaches of his imagination, or in the process of restoring old movie theaters, had he ever expected to come across anything like this.

They obviously had reason for being there, he mused as he sat back on his heels. If the poster he'd seen on display at the Beaumont Hotel were any criteria, these were worth their weight in gold.

T.J. gingerly worked at the wall again. Unless he was wrong, there had to be more posters between the exterior and interior walls. From the condition of the mildewed wall, some of the posters were probably water damaged, but with the hot, dry climate, others would still have to be in good condition.

As to why they were in between the walls, as an experienced restoration builder and architect, he was pretty sure of the answer. They had to have been used as a cheap means of insulation when the Great Depression of the Thirties had hit, and the economy took a dive. Builders of the time had gone bankrupt and undoubtedly used whatever cheap material they could find.

As an amateur film historian, he knew somewhere there had to be a historical society who had blueprints that could prove his theory.

He also remembered there had been talk of making the Venice canal and the surrounding real estate into a designated historical area. When nothing had come of it, most of the land had been sold and turned into condominiums like the one next door for the new, wealthy cyberspace generation. If someone didn't intervene, Emily's cottage would surely suffer the same fate.

The important thing was if there were more posters between the walls, Emily would surely be a wealthy woman. And what would she decide to do if he told her what he'd found?

Chapter Twelve

The sound of a refrigerator door closing roused T.J. from his reverie. Any further search behind the walls would have to wait.

He made up his mind not to give Emily false hopes until he had a chance to tear down the interior bedroom wall and take a good look inside. If it turned out the walls actually hid more posters, he'd tell her then. The truth was, if Emily knew about the posters, he was afraid she would sell out and be on her way.

He dusted off his jeans, glanced over at the window to make sure it was securely locked and headed for the kitchen.

"Ready?"

Emily smiled and motioned to the plate of ham and cheese sandwiches and a fresh pot of steaming coffee. "I'm sorry it's not more elaborate, but this is all I had in the house."

"Good enough." T.J. crossed the kitchen and

planted a kiss on the tip of Emily's nose. "I have an idea. How about taking a break after breakfast."

Emily glanced at the door to the hall that led to her bedroom, rolled her eyes and shrugged. The day was young. The next item on *her* agenda would have to wait. "A break?"

"Sure. How about going to the carnival this afternoon." He pulled out the brochure he had in his back pocket. "I'm pretty sure I know how you feel about carnivals, sweetheart, and today is the last day. So how about putting on your costume, Miss Dorothy, and grabbing Toto. In broad daylight, and with me keeping you company, you have nothing to worry about."

"It's much prettier under the stars and the moonlight," she answered wistfully, glancing through the kitchen window at the late afternoon sunshine. "But I'm game if you are. Did you bring your pirate's costume with you?"

"Not this time." He grinned and reached for a sandwich. "When you called, all I could think of was the urgency in your voice and how fast I could get over here. If you think I need a costume, I have my tool belt in the truck. I can go as a carpenter."

Emily nodded. "Have you decided what to do about the bedroom wall?"

"Yep, but it will have to wait a while. It's going to take more than a simple fix to do the job. I'll have to get the company involved." T.J. chewed thoughtfully and took a swallow of coffee. "We probably need a new roof. I'm sorry, but it's going to take a while."

"Did you say 'we'?"

"Yes, I did," he answered. "You haven't forgotten I offered to buy the cottage, have you?" She shook her head. "After my company puts the cottage back into its original condition, I plan on giving it back to you as a wedding present."

"It's a little too soon to talk about wedding presents, don't you think? We're not even married." Emily gathered the empty cups and plates and sighed. "There are still things I have to think about. What will I do if it rains?"

T.J. glanced out the kitchen window. "Not to worry. There isn't a cloud in the sky." He eyed her sandwich. "If you're not going to eat that, I still have a powerful hunger."

She pushed the plate toward him. "Me, too." She grinned and started for the sink. "But I guess I'll have to settle for the carnival."

T.J. felt guilty as hell. It was tell the truth and risk losing her, or wait and see what materialized. Between a rock and a hard place, he decided to get Emily out of the cottage until he had a chance to persuade her to move in with him.

"It's not too soon for me, sweetheart." T.J. followed her to the sink. When she turned around, he put his arms around her and nibbled at her ear. She smelled of coffee, ham and cheese, and darned if she didn't taste a heck of a lot better than the real thing. "By the way, Em, how about moving in with me until the repairs are made?"

Emily hesitated. It wasn't easy to make up her mind about something so important as moving in with T.J. "I hadn't thought of leaving here yet, Tom. At least, not yet. As for getting married, I'm not sure I'm ready to make up my mind. I have some decisions to make."

T.J. ran a finger across her lips. "I know. I know I haven't courted you properly. And that maybe I still have something to prove." He moved on to caress the side of her neck. "I still have high hopes, sweetheart. Until then, would you rather I stayed here with you? I can always sleep on the couch."

She gazed at him in a way that made his mouth go dry and his knees turn to rubber. "Is that a real commitment, Tom?"

Realizing she was afraid he would change his mind, T.J. nodded and lifted her chin so that their lips could meet. Deep within, he knew that the next few moments would determine the path the rest of his life would take. "You bet! Just give me a chance to prove it to you."

"You're sure?"

"I'm sure," he answered. "But rather than rushing you, how about our taking that break and going out to enjoy the carnival?"

"I'll get dressed." T.J.'s heart beat faster when he saw the stars shining in her eyes. Was it the prospect of the carnival or moving in with him that put the stars there?

He held his breath. Maybe he was being selfish. Maybe he should have told her about the posters before he proposed their moving in together. The awful truth was that it was probably too late.

If he was right about the value of the hidden posters, Emily could live out any dream she'd ever had from day one. And any other dreams she might come up with in the future.

As if that thought wasn't enough to tear him apart, he had a bigger problem to worry about. Would she still want to marry him when she had to finally confront the truth about his real identity?

It served him right. For letting Emily's attractions get in the way. He should have insisted on proving he wasn't Tim from the get-go and still have offered to help her. He'd been raised to tell the truth, the whole truth and nothing but the truth, hadn't he? And yet, the first time he'd come face-to-face with a real choice, he'd chosen to perpetuate a lie.

He heard Emily singing "Over the Rainbow," a sweet, nostalgic song that wished dreams would come true. He closed his eyes and prayed for guidance to any saint who had some spare time to hear him.

An hour later, to his relief, he was enjoying the

carnival and even more pleasing, the sound of Emily's laughter. A toddler ran into his leg. With a laugh, T.J. lifted the boy into the air and handed him to his mother. Instead of being angry at her son for running away, the mother smiled her thanks and hugged the kid. Just the kind of kid he hoped he and Emily would have some day, he thought with a side glance at Emily's rapt expression.

Before long, he was holding a shopping bag containing a tissue-wrapped papier-mâché mask in one hand and a bag of Italian pastry in the other. The mask was for Emily because it reminded her of Italy. The cream-filled puff pastry was for him. To his chagrin, there wasn't a pastry he could willingly pass up.

Emily carried her plush terrier Toto and munched on a cone of pink cotton candy. Like the character she portrayed, her auburn hair was parted in the middle and gathered on each side with bright red ribbons. Her eyes shone with happiness.

She made a perfect Dorothy for a perfect day, T.J. mused contentedly as they walked alongside the canal where multicolored lights were reflected in the water. Like her motion picture counterpart, she was eager to discover just what came next over the rainbow. Walking beside her, he was surprised to feel younger and more carefree than he had in years.

Maybe it was coming to grips with his adoption that had lessened the burden of his perceived re-

sponsibilities. His father's assurance that T.J. had
nothing to prove certainly helped. Or maybe it was
Emily's love and devotion. In any case, he'd finally
turned his head around and put the past behind him
where it belonged. Maybe he was a better man for
doing it.

He smiled fondly over at Emily. She was licking
the sweet pink spun sugar confection off her lips and
sent his body and thoughts into overdrive. He
couldn't help himself. If ever a woman's lips were
meant to be kissed, they had to be Emily's. And if
ever there was a woman who could balance his
workaholic and pragmatic personality with an ide-
alistic view of the world, it was Emily. And that
was all right with him.

He glanced up at the darkening sky in time to
glimpse the first star to appear on the horizon.

At seven, he'd searched the heavens for the first
star to appear. He wished then that his mother would
come back for him and his younger brother so they
wouldn't have to continue to live in foster homes.
No one seemed to want older children. The wish had
partially come true but not the way he'd expected.
His mother hadn't returned, but he'd been blessed
with wonderful new parents and a life any kid would
have envied, adopted or not. In hindsight, he should
have thanked his lucky star and never looked back
at his troubled past.

Tonight, his wish upon the first star he'd glimpse

was going to be about hoping to persuade Emily to believe in him.

Gazing up at the star, he found himself softly reciting the familiar jingle. "Star light, star bright, the first star I see tonight I wish I may I wish I might have the wish I wish tonight."

Emily paused in midbite and sidestepped a Harlequin and his lady who were too engrossed in each other to watch where they were going. It was a moment before she was able to come back to his side. "Did you say something, Tom?"

At first, T.J. felt foolish for having spoken the jingle aloud. Until he gazed into Emily's questioning hazel eyes. Where was it written that a man couldn't be sentimental and still be manly when he was with the woman he loved?

"I wished upon a star," he said casually. "Just a kid's game." He hoped she wouldn't laugh at him.

"I always wish on the first star I see, too," she confessed with a shy grin. "If you tell me your wish, I'll tell you mine."

"Promise you won't laugh?"

She nodded and crossed her heart. "I promise."

"You've got yourself a deal," he answered even as he knew he couldn't give away the wish. Gazing down at Emily's star-filled eyes, he wanted to believe there would be years of tomorrows ahead for them. Days filled with her presence and the sounds of children. Nights filled with Emily in his arms while he showed her how precious she was to him. He glanced up at the star and took a chance on making a second silent wish. This time he wished that everything between them would turn out the way he hoped.

"I wished for a large dose of moonlight," he compromised. "A dozen more stars and years of private moments with you."

She brushed her fingers against his lips and smiled into her eyes. "You'll never know how much you touch my heart, Tom."

"Emily!"

To T.J.'s chagrin, a loud voice broke into the warm rapport that had fallen between himself and Emily. He glanced over his shoulder to see a vaguely familiar man push his way through the crowded walk and head toward them. The guy looked vaguely familiar.

"Hold up there a minute, Emily! I want to talk to you."

As the man got closer, T.J. recognized Emily's former fiancé. His warm feeling vanished in the blink of an eye. The guy's timing sure stank.

Emily's rapt smile disappeared. "I'm afraid it's Sean, my ex-fiancé. I have to talk to him."

T.J. recalled the scene back at the Beaumont when he'd seen the man embrace Emily, and he gritted his teeth. He'd have to hear her dream later. "Go ahead, but remember I'm here if you need me."

Sean cast a surly glance at T.J., then, to T.J.'s annoyance, turned his back on him. "I had a hell of a time finding you, Emily. I thought you were going to call me so we could make some plans about our wedding."

"I was in a hurry to leave the hotel." Emily answered with a glance at T.J. "How did you know where to find me?"

"After I told your lawyer's secretary I was your fiancé, she told me where to find you. She also told me you were married and had your husband with you." He glowered at T.J. "I set her straight. Is this the guy she was talking about?"

"T.J., this is Sean Foster," she said to Tom, ignoring Sean's question. "A man I used to know."

"*Used to know?*" Sean sputtered. "*Engaged to,* is more like it."

"Were engaged," Emily said firmly. "But that's over and done with. I'm sorry, I should have told you we were through before I checked out at the Beaumont."

"Like hell!"

T.J. took a threatening step toward Sean.

"So, who is this guy?" he sneered. "The husband?"

"A friend. A good friend."

"A friend?" Sean echoed suggestively. "That's not what I heard. Hell, I heard you've already spent the night together. We have to talk somewhere private.''

''There's nothing more to talk about, Sean. I'm not about to change my mind.''

T.J. fought to keep his cool for Emily's sake, but it wasn't easy. He sure as hell didn't like the sexual innuendo or the proprietary way Sean looked at Emily. He added Sean to the list of people who riled the hell out of him. A list headed by Daniels and now Daniels's secretary, Maggie. From the way it sounded, she was ready to give away Emily's current whereabouts to anyone who'd asked for it. All the more reason to persuade Emily to let him move in with her.

Sean bit his lower lip and shot daggers at T.J. ''We still have to talk.''

Emily shook her head. ''Go home, Sean. Go home and forget me.''

T.J. wasn't surprised to hear Emily tell her ex-fiancé off. But he *was* surprised she hadn't gone on to tell the guy about his own marriage proposal. Hadn't she believed him when he'd told her he loved her and wanted to be her husband?

Sean pierced T.J. with a sour look that made T.J.'s fists curl. ''In case you have any ideas about making this 'husband' of yours a real one, maybe you'd better think again. Just what do you know about this guy?''

"Enough to know T.J. is an honest man. Someone I can depend on."

T.J. felt like a heel. How honest was he when he was masquerading as his brother? And hiding this discovery of the movie posters—at least for now? The answer was clear. He wasn't.

Emily tossed the unfinished paper cone of cotton candy into a trash container, scaring away a pair of hungry seagulls. "My relationship with T.J. has nothing to do with you. As for our engagement, it was over the day you walked out on me."

Sean flushed at the reminder.

T.J. smothered an urge to hit him.

With a baleful look, Sean turned on his heel and disappeared into the crowd.

T.J. bit back a comment when he saw a sad look on Emily's face as she gazed after Sean. He realized she wasn't the type of person to willingly hurt anyone, and she was vulnerable enough to be hurt herself. He hated himself even more than ever. If anyone needed to talk straight to Emily, it was him.

But not tonight. There was no use in ruining the carnival. Not when tonight was the first night of his and Emily's new relationship. Tonight belonged to himself and Emily.

He noticed an ersatz gondolier dressed in a red-and-green-striped T-shirt, black pants and a wide-brimmed black sailor's hat hustling business. The man might not be the real thing and the canal only a sorry imitation of the canals in Italy, but they were better than nothing. At least the gondolas had been decorated with red and green flags and balloons and looked real enough.

The stars shining overhead had to be as beautiful as the stars shining over Italy, he mused as he looked up at the sky. And, miracle of miracles, the gondolier began to sing an Italian love song.

Suddenly, a series of fireworks shot into the air. While he watched, streaks of light arched across the darkening horizon and burst into sprays of multicolored stars. He glanced at Emily's wistful expression. "Gondola ride, Em?"

The words seemed to be magic; Emily came to life. Her blossoming smile brought a smile to his heart. "This was your wish, wasn't it, Em?"

She nodded happily. "I thought you'd never ask."

"Didn't you ever take gondola rides here before?" He fingered one of the red ribbons in her moonlight-lit hair. What he really wanted to do was to take her home where he could hold her, make love to her and make her forget the Seans of the world. A place where he could make her believe they were the only two people in the universe. A place where no one would ever hurt her again, including him. First, he had to make tonight's dream come true.

"Oh yes. At carnival time with my aunt. But even

at twelve, I knew it would be more exciting and certainly more romantic if I were in a gondola with the man I love.''

"Then, I'm your man," he called to the gondolier to hold up.

The smiling gondolier handed Emily into the swaying craft. T.J. left their packages on the canal's edge and gingerly followed her into the long, narrow vessel, curved at both ends. With a wink and a flourish, the gondolier handed T.J. a light knit throw to put over their laps then stationed himself on a wooden slat at the rear of the small vessel. At a push with a long wooden paddle, the gondola began to glide through the dark, blue-green salt water flowing into the canal from the ocean. Overhead, the stars twinkled. The gondolier burst into a new love song.

T.J. put an arm around Emily and drew her close. "Happy?"

Emily curled her fingers through his. "I always knew it could be like this," she said contentedly. "But back then I thought that if this ever happened, it would have to be in another time and place and maybe, another lifetime. Maybe in Italy."

"Why Italy, why not here?" T.J. nuzzled Emily's sweet-smelling hair and hugged her close. It seemed to him that he fell more in love with Emily with every passing moment and that he'd never felt so contented, so at peace with himself as now.

"Because Sean didn't believe in fairy tales."

"The guy must be missing a few of his marbles," T.J. muttered. What man could resist believing in fairy tales when they were the dreams of a woman he supposedly loved?

"Maybe. He said they were fairy tales and that fairy tales were for children."

"Forget him," T.J. whispered, and turned her head up to meet his. "You have me now. I swear I not only believe in fairy tales, I believe in you."

He captured her lips as they glided under a bridge. When she put her arms around his neck and fervently kissed him back, he heard the gondolier murmur, *"bravissimo."*

Emily knew even fairy tales had to have an ending, but the gondola ride to the end of the canal and back was over too soon to suit her. The mystical experience had been a dream come true, she thought as T.J. paid the gondolier and added a generous tip. Just as T.J. had been the perfect partner to share the dream.

Dreams should have happy endings, but she knew that sooner or later she would have to face reality.

The last two weeks, since she'd "bought" Tom at an auction had been full of surprises. Moving into the cottage had brought back memories that stirred her very soul and awakened the woman in her. She'd not only fallen in love with him, she was thinking of moving in with him. An idea so unlike her.

Everything had happened so quickly, she knew she had to have time to sort out her thoughts.

"Home again?" T.J. murmured. He put his arm around her shoulders to shelter her from the damp air coming across the ocean. "We could take up where we left off. I'd love to wake up in the morning with you in my arms."

Moving in together would be a giant step. First, she had to make certain it would be not only for tonight but for tomorrow and always. She couldn't settle for less.

Before she could answer, Sean moved back into view.

"Look, Emily. Maybe I came across like gangbusters before and I'm sorry. I've come back to apologize." He glanced warily at T.J. "I'd still like to talk to you alone."

"You can come back to the cottage for coffee, if you like," she said with an apologetic glance at T.J. "But..."

No sooner were the words out of her mouth, than T.J. had stepped between her and Sean.

"Not on your life!" he said. "What's the point, anyway?"

"The point, Mr. Kirkpatrick," Sean spat, "is that Emily and I go back a long way. I have the right to talk to her. As far as I can tell, she's only known you for a few weeks, if that long."

"How long we've known each other has nothing

to do with it!'' T.J. answered. ''You had your chance, and you blew it!''

''At least I didn't go around telling everyone I was Emily's husband,'' Sean rejoined. ''What's the matter, are you after her inheritance?''

T.J. was almost speechless. Sure as hell, he was guilty of pretending to be Emily's husband, but not by choice. He'd only intended to do Emily a favor after his brother had lit out on her, hadn't he? Falling in love with Emily had been serendipitous, and he didn't intend to apologize to anyone. As far as being after her inheritance, the idea was ridiculous.

''That's none of your business,'' he answered, his fists curled. ''Get lost!''

Emily elbowed her way between the two men. Her heart told her T.J. did love her, but he *was* practically a stranger. All the more reason for taking time out to sort through her thoughts.

''That's enough! The idea of both of you fighting over me is ludicrous and I won't put up with it. Sean, go home and don't come back.''

When Sean turned on his heel and stomped off, Emily turned to T.J. ''I'm sorry, T.J. All of this nonsense has given me a raging headache. Why don't we call it a night?''

Chapter Thirteen

After a sleepless night, Emily's heart still ached. Not because T.J. and Sean had argued over her, or the look on T.J.'s face when she'd said good-night, but because Sean had been right about her not knowing T.J.

She knew T.J. had been adopted after an unhappy early childhood. That he was a partner in a building restoration firm bearing his name. That he was a romantic lover and was a believer in dreams, including hers.

He also was thirty-something with a smile that most women would kill for and yet had still managed to remain single. A man who'd admitted he hadn't believed in or considered marriage until he met her, she mused unhappily as she showered and dressed. But was that enough?

Considering one man had already jilted her for a more desirable woman, she found it difficult to believe T.J. loved her enough to marry her after knowing her for two weeks.

Although she'd managed to fall in love with him, his abrupt change of mind had continued to bother her, even before Sean's parting comment. How could she love a man who'd confessed to avoiding lasting relationships? How could she be sure he wouldn't change his mind again?

More to the point, she asked herself as she shrugged into a blue linen pantsuit, had she fallen in love with the real man, or a fantasy man she'd created?

The sound of T.J.'s phone, which he'd left behind, awakened her from her musings.

"Em?"

"Yes." The sound of T.J.'s deep voice and use of her pet name sent a warmth coursing through her. She forgot the questions she wanted to ask.

"I just got a message that Daniels is back in town and wants to meet with us today. I knew you wanted to get things over with, so I called ahead for an appointment. Say, about two o'clock. Is that okay with you?"

"I'll be ready." She said goodbye and clicked off the cell phone. The sooner she put the business of her inheritance behind her, the sooner she could get on with her life. Perhaps, even a life without the man she loved.

She'd wandered onto the cottage porch when T.J.

drove up. Instead of his weathered pickup, he was driving a new silver Lexus. His appearance, as he strode toward her, had changed. From the casual jeans, T-shirt and sweater of yesterday, he was wearing beige linen slacks and a jacket over a silk short-sleeved olive shirt. His shoes were brown slip-ons instead of sturdy leather boots.

He looked all male, dressed to kill and ready for business. His gaze was polite, but she missed the twinkle in his eyes and his ready smile. He was the man who had made her come alive, made her believe they had a future together. For all that, he was a man she really didn't know.

"Ready?"

She nodded, took her purse from off the swing and locked the cottage door behind her. There was no use in remembering the wonderful way he'd made love to her. No use in thinking about a future with him. It was *safer* to stick to business for now.

T.J. was silent on their way to the lawyer's office, but as far as he was concerned, his relationship with Emily was unfinished business. He just had to find a way make her believe him.

To add to his mental turmoil, Emily hadn't answered him about their moving in together. The way things were stacking up now, his chances were slim to none.

He wasn't a man to quit when he believed in something.

The faint scent of lavender that clung to Emily's clothing turned his thoughts to the night they'd spent together. He'd been left breathless by her uninhibited response and wanted more before he'd take a break. Deep in his soul, he wanted to share her life, her hopes, her dreams. To spend the rest of his life making both their dreams come true.

He glanced over at Emily. The unhappy look on her face mirrored his own troubled thoughts. After he'd gotten the message Daniels had called, his sixth sense had warned him there was big trouble brewing. The only consolation he took from the moment was knowing that since he was already in deep trouble, there was nowhere to go but up.

The drive from the beach to Daniels's downtown office took twenty-five minutes, but to T.J., it was more like a lifetime. He'd needed to talk to Emily, to explain one more time, he was a changed man since he'd met her. That he wasn't Tim, and to persuade her the past wasn't going to get in the way of their future.

He pulled into the underground parking lot of the cold marble building. What awaited him upstairs?

Maggie, Daniels's secretary, greeted them with a wide-eyed too-innocent look. "Go right in, Mr. Kirkpatrick. Mr. Daniels is waiting for you."

T.J. smothered a curse. His premonition something was wrong was right on the button or Maggie wouldn't have been so formal. He strode into the office with Emily at his back.

Daniels rose from his large mahogany desk, a studied smile on his face. T.J. ignored his outstretched hand. After what Noel had told him about Daniels's reputation, he wasn't about to be friendly. "Let's get on with it!"

Daniels dropped his hand and gestured to the two leather armchairs in front of his desk. "Please, have a seat."

With a cool glance at Daniels, Emily sat down. T.J. sat down beside her.

"Before we start, Miss Holmes," the lawyer said amiably. "Are you sure you want Mr. Kirkpatrick to remain here?" She nodded.

"Then let's begin. I want to inform you that while I was away my staff did some research into your aunt's property."

T.J. started. "What kind of research?"

Emily stared at the lawyer. "Does that include prowling around the cottage and questioning neighbors?"

Daniels shrugged. "Research of all kinds is part of the business to insure the proper transfer of estates."

"I've done some research of my own, Mr. Daniels." She added quietly. "I have it on good authority that, since I am my aunt's sole legal survivor, the property is mine. Married or not."

T.J. admired Emily's direct challenge, especially when the lawyer's face registered anger. The guy might think he was clever, but he wasn't wise enough to understand vulnerable people weren't stupid. Just trusting.

"Of course," Daniels answered smoothly with a quick glance at T.J. "As an old friend of your Aunt Emily's, I was merely trying to honor her last wish to see to it you were protected."

Emily looked surprised. "I never knew that you were a friend of hers. Aunt Emily never mentioned you."

T.J. read Emily's expression, even if Daniels didn't. If the lawyer had been such a good friend of her late aunt, why was he trying to put one over on Emily?

Daniels frowned. "Indeed," he answered coolly. "Actually, we knew each other off and on for many years. I'm sure that's why she asked me to handle her will. The marriage provision was inserted because she felt if you were married at the time she passed away, there would be no chance of some fortune hunter latching on to you." He glanced meaningfully at T.J., then back at Emily.

T.J. shot forward in his seat. "Watch it, Daniels. I might have riled up a person or two in my career, but I've never been called a fortune hunter."

Emily smiled wearily, rubbed her forehead and reached into her purse for a roll of peppermints.

"Mr. Daniels, Aunt Emily told me many times that she wished I was married, so the clause didn't come as a surprise. Although I doubt that a seventy-year-old cottage would be considered a fortune."

Daniels sat back in his executive chair and smiled. T.J. was tempted to wipe the smile off his face. "Maybe, maybe not. But first things first, my dear. Are we all agreed that you and Mr. Kirkpatrick are not man and wife?"

T.J. met Daniels' gaze. "You know damn well we're not. Why bother to ask?"

Daniels held up the business card T.J. had given to Maggie. "Are you or are you not T. J. Kirkpatrick? Thomas Jefferson Kirkpatrick?"

T.J. tensed for what was coming next. Damn! He'd intended to tell Emily the truth today, but it was too late.

"I am." T.J. reached for Emily's cold hand. He knew his answer was about to hit the fan and hoped to cushion what was coming next. Now that the issue of Emily's marital state was no longer in question, T.J. sensed the lawyer still intended to get back at him for championing Emily.

"Are you or are you not the man Miss Holmes hired to pose as her husband? The man who was in the photograph she presented as proof she was married?"

His stomach in knots, T.J. waited for the other shoe to drop.

"I ask you again, Mr. Kirkpatrick. Are you the same man Miss Holmes claimed to be her husband, or are you merely his stand-in?"

T.J. thought fast. If Emily learned he'd been living a lie, would it help to explain he'd only wanted to help her after Tim had chickened out? That he'd never expected to gain something for his efforts?

The office was thick with unspoken accusations.

"I take it from your silence that you're not the same man." Daniels smiled his satisfaction as he glanced down at T.J.'s business card. "It wasn't easy, but research turned up that interesting fact." He consulted his notes. "*I* have it on good authority it was your brother, Timothy, Miss Holmes 'hired' at a bachelor's charity auction. And that he is the man in the photograph she presented on her first visit here."

T.J. grasped Emily's hand more tightly. He answered the lawyer, but he gazed into her eyes as he spoke. Strangely enough, she didn't look shocked, not even close. When had she known the truth? Why had she gone along with him, slept with him, if she knew he wasn't Tim?

"I tried to tell Emily right away I wasn't the man she'd bid on and won at the auction. I tried to tell her my brother and I looked enough alike to be twins. Emily needed help and, strangely enough, didn't seem to want to believe me."

He put his love for her in his gaze as he directed

the rest of his answer to her. "After I listened to your story, Em, I realized someone had to help you. One look into your eyes that afternoon and I knew that someone was going to be me. What I didn't realize at the time, was that I'd already fallen in love with you."

He turned his anger on the lawyer. "Emily's problem was the one you created in the first place by lying to her about the will. Not because I tried to help out in Tim's place. If you'd told the truth, none of this would have happened."

He glanced back at Emily. It damn near broke his heart to see the hurt in her eyes. Of the three men in her life, all three had lied to her. Or, in his case at least, had hidden the truth.

"Miss Holmes?"

"Leave her alone!" With a staying glance at Emily, T.J. jumped to his feet. "I've already admitted who I am. But I swear it has nothing to do with Emily's inheritance."

"I'm afraid it does," Daniels retorted, satisfaction oozing from him like glue from a bottle. "According to what my staff has managed to discover, you and Miss Holmes are practically strangers. She may claim her inheritance, but for her sake, I feel she needs to know just what kind of man you are."

Emily took her hand from T.J.'s and folded it in her lap. "I know what kind of a man Mr. Kirkpatrick is. He tried to tell me his identity, and while I didn't believe him at the time, I think subconsciously I must have known the truth. I needed help, and something about him told me he was the man who could help me. Besides, I'd already fallen in love with him." She smiled sadly at T.J. "No matter what else he's done or who he actually is, he has helped me in more ways than he knows."

T.J. touched her cheek in gratitude. He realized how hard it had been for her to admit to things she had never admitted before. Let alone in front of Daniels. He faced Daniels. "Now that my identity is out in the open, what's the point of going on with this?"

"Merely to show Miss Holmes you aren't the man she thought you were. And to demonstrate to her why her aunt wanted her to be married."

Emily rose to leave. "What I chose to believe then isn't important now. Legally, my aunt's property belongs to me. If you have any papers for me to sign, I would appreciate signing them now."

"We're not quite through yet," Daniels replied. He glanced down at an open folder lying on his desk. "There's the matter of the value of the estate. In particular, the cottage on the property."

T.J. recognized the letterhead of the County Building and Safety Land Development Office. He'd seen inspection reports often enough to imagine what it contained. He hid a shudder and prayed that his worst nightmare wasn't about to come true. "Spit it out. What else?"

"There's a little matter of a rumor that has been going around the building industry for years. In fact, when the cottage on the adjoining property was razed, it seems the rumor turned out to be true." He gestured to the report on his desk. "At least, to some degree. And if I'm not mistaken…" He left the sentence unfinished at T.J.'s muttered curse.

"That's enough!" T.J. retorted, on his feet and leaning over the desk. "Again, the rumor has nothing to do with Emily. Give her the papers and let her sign and let us get out of here."

Privately, T.J.'s heart sank. It was beginning to look as if Daniels had done more than come up with T.J.'s identity during his research. The rumor he'd referred to had to be about any vintage motion picture posters that may have been discovered when the cottage next door had been razed. The same type of poster he'd discovered behind the wall in her aunt's bedroom. Living in Placerville, Emily couldn't have known about them. But why would Daniels bring it up now? And what would Emily believe if he did?

He only had himself to blame. As soon as he'd glimpsed the posters, he should have done some research of his own.

More to the point, he should have had enough faith in Emily's love for him to tell her of his find. He should have told her then instead of waiting for the right moment. He'd been around long enough to know that sometimes the right moment never came.

"I don't know what you're driving at, Mr. Daniels," Emily interrupted, "but I've had enough of this conversation. I don't want to hear any more about Mr. Kirkpatrick. He has nothing to do with my inheritance. The estate belongs to me and me alone. I insist I be allowed to sign the documents that transfer it to me. And I want to do it now."

"Of course." With a murderous look at T.J., Daniels picked up a legal document and pushed it to the edge of the desk. "I only felt it was my duty to point out the dangers inherent in your becoming a wealthy woman. If you like, we can discuss this again later." He pointed to the line for her signature. "Additionally, you understand that there will be my fee and a matter of taxes when title is transferred?"

Emily took the pen he offered and blindly signed on the line he marked with an X. "Send me a bill. And please see that I get a copy of the deed." She turned on her heel and walked out of the office.

T.J. followed with a withering glance at Daniels. He wasn't going to let Emily out of his sight until he had a chance to explain why he hadn't told Emily about the old movie posters. Before she discovered them for herself.

HOME AGAIN, and finally alone, Emily made her way to her aunt's bedroom. If ever she needed to feel her aunt's loving presence, it was now. She needed comfort, just as she'd so often sought comfort when she had been a young girl.

She sank into the rocking chair, closed her eyes and leaned her head against the wooden back. With a small push of her shoe, she set it rocking.

"Aunt Emily," she whispered. "I don't know what to do. Sell the property or stay here? After today, I don't even know who to trust."

The air seemed to thicken. A warmth filled the room. Emily imagined a gentle hand brush her cheek.

She turned her face into the imagined hand. "I'm sorry to disappoint you, Aunt Emily," she whispered. "I'm not married, but I did fall in love twice. And both times with men who couldn't be trusted. I guess you'll just have to put up with me the way I am."

With a sign, Emily opened her eyes. Even though T.J. had taught her life was for the taking, she couldn't bring herself to imagine a new life without him.

Her gaze lingered on the mildewed wall. The same wall T.J. had been inspecting when she'd asked him to leave off his inspection, come back to bed keep her warm. He'd left a small opening behind him.

It might have been the beam of sunshine coming through the lace curtains at the window, but it appeared as if the room seemed to light up. She looked around the room for something to use to work on the wall and focused on the brass letter opener beside the bed. She took the opener and chipped away at the damp plaster until another section broke loose to reveal a cardboard movie poster. She took a deep breath and looked inside.

To her surprise, she caught a glimpse of a poster advertising the 1939 movie, *The Wizard of Oz.* A duplicate of the poster she'd seen on display earlier at the Beaumont Hotel.

Her excitement grew when she recalled the poster at the hotel had been advertised for auction at Sotheby's with a starting bid of $9,000.

Excited now, she loosened another small section of the plaster wall. This time, she found a vintage poster advertising Greta Garbo as Mata Hari. The value of the poster was unknown to her, but the poster alongside it was that of *The Adventures of Robin Hood.* The face of the hero, Errol Flynn, smiled jauntily back at her.

Emily sank down on the floor and covered her lips with a trembling hand. Surely the posters had to be worth as much as the poster she'd coveted that depicted Dorothy, the Tin Man, the Cowardly Lion, and the Straw Man dancing arm in arm up the Yellow Brick Road. This must have been the fortune Daniels had hinted at!

She heard Daniels's voice accusing T.J. of romancing her for her "fortune." She remembered T.J. had offered more than once to buy the cottage. He'd been the one to break into the mildewed wall on the pretext of checking the wall for damage. And he'd kept his silence.

She gazed back at the posters. It didn't take a stretch of her imagination to decide T.J. had known there was a small fortune in back of the wall.

"Emily?"

She swung around to face T.J. He was in the bedroom doorway, his body tense, his face as white as the surrounding doorjamb he leaned against.

"I was hoping to get here before you found the posters." He slowly came into the room and stopped at the side of the rocking chair. "I wanted to be the one to tell you about them."

By now, Emily didn't know what or who to believe. But she did know T.J. had used her for some purpose of his own. She looked at his stricken face, the hopelessness in his gaze. "This is what Daniels was trying to tell me when he said that you were a fortune hunter. Wasn't it?"

"Only part of what you believe is true," he answered. "I found a poster the other day, but I had no intention of keeping it from you."

"Why?" she said simply. "Why would you not have told me?"

"I was afraid that if you knew about the posters, you might change your mind about marrying me. I was half-afraid you'd fallen for me on the rebound, anyway. I was even afraid you'd sell out and go off to Italy."

"So you offered to buy the property for yourself, hoping I'd never find out the truth. Or, if I did, would find it out too late. Is that it?"

"Never," he answered. "You have to believe me. I wanted us to get married. I'd hoped to restore the cottage and put it back in its original state for you. I wanted to give it to you as a belated wedding present."

When Emily rose and backed away from him, T.J. felt a hollow dread in the pit of his stomach. She wasn't listening. He would have given his right arm not to have put the anguish in her eyes. If he didn't know better, he thought his heart would break.

He had to try again. "I never would have kept the posters for myself, Em. I swear. I didn't even know they were here when I first offered to buy the cottage from you."

"If you didn't know about the posters, why would you care if I sold it to someone else?" She brushed her hair out of her eyes. It was all he could do not to try to take her in his arms and kiss away the hurt in her eyes.

"Because I've spent the past twenty years restoring vintage buildings. The moment I saw this one, I fell in love with it. I knew it was a prime example of fine craftsmanship and priceless materials.

"I only knew you intended to sell the property," he went on. "I couldn't stand the idea that the cottage would be bulldozed to make way for another condo complex like the one next door."

Emily crossed her arms around herself to hold back the pain. T.J.'s hopeful smile would have broken her heart, if she had a whole heart to break.

"It's not only the posters," she said sadly. "When you knew I thought you were the man I'd bid on and won at the auction, you went along with the subterfuge. You let me fall in love with you."

She toyed with the brass letter opener and replaced it on the nightstand. "I don't know who or what to believe anymore. But I do know I've had enough of men who tell lies. Men I can't trust."

Emily's admission that she loved him was enough for him not to give her up without another try. He took a step toward her for one last chance to convince her they belonged together. "Emily, please listen to me. I never intended to hurt you or take anything from you. I swear I love you for yourself."

She shook her head. "It's too late. Please, do us both a favor and leave."

Chapter Fourteen

If there was one thing T.J. recognized, it was a hurt woman. Not because he'd had any firsthand experience along those lines, but because he'd seen his brother Tim break female hearts since he was old enough to like girls.

T.J. knew he'd been a damn fool to hurt Emily, intentionally or otherwise.

He should have known better. He wasn't a fool to have fallen in love with her, but for underestimating the kind of woman she was. She was true-blue, honest and loyal. The kind of woman who played for keeps. A sensitive woman whose vulnerability was one reason he treasured her so much.

He should have recognized Emily as the woman for him from the first moment he'd gazed into those incredibly trusting hazel eyes.

He knew he didn't deserve her, but that wasn't going to stop him from loving her. One way or another, he had to prove he was the man for her. To somehow show her he was willing to share any dreams she might have—past, present or future. And that meant swallowing his pride and going back to talk to Emily.

Seagulls glided overhead, croaking warning calls as he rang the old-fashioned doorbell. He didn't care. He had nothing to lose except Emily, and he didn't intend to lose her.

Instead of chimes, he heard the tinkling notes of the bittersweet song, "Over the Rainbow." The haunting melody sung by Judy Garland in the motion picture *The Wizard of Oz,* which remained popular more than sixty years later. No wonder Emily had grown up dreaming of someday flying over the rainbow to Italy.

All the more reason he wanted to know if there were other dreams Emily hadn't mentioned.

Dressed in the blue slip dress she'd worn the first time he'd noticed her, Emily came to the door and peered through the screen. His body reacted just as it had reacted the first time he'd seen her wearing the dress. If there hadn't been a screen door between them, he would have had her in his arms and kissed their differences away.

"Good," T.J. said, with a sigh of relief. "I'm glad you're still here."

He'd been half-afraid Emily had already hightailed it back up north to Placerville.

"I'm waiting on a copy of the will. I want to be

sure Daniels filed it before I leave.'' The screen door remained closed. ''Why are you here?''

''I've been thinking. May I come in?'' When she hesitated, he tried a smile. ''No farther than the living room couch, I promise.''

The screen door creaked on its hinges as Emily opened it to let him in and gestured to the couch. ''What's on your mind?''

Gingerly he sat down on the old-fashioned mohair couch. He shifted uncomfortably when the short bristles dug into the back of his bare legs. ''I was wondering if you'd ever stopped to think we were destined to meet?''

Emily eyed T.J.'s discomfiture. He was back to wearing khaki safari shorts and a sleeveless T-shirt and looked more like the sexy man she remembered at the building site two weeks ago. That was the trouble with the Kirkpatrick men, she mused uneasily as a renegade warmth stole over her. They were sexier than they had any right to be.

She had to do something to get away from his searching eyes before she gave in to her yearning to be in his arms. ''Wait here a minute,'' she said. ''I'll be right back.''

T.J. stirred restlessly against the stiff bristles and wistfully eyed the red velvet cushions on the window seat. After sampling the couch, no wonder Emily had spent countless hours curled up on the soft velvet pillows gazing out the large picture window.

He knew now that whenever he thought of Emily, he would picture her there, against the velvet cushions, dreaming the childhood dreams that masked the unhappiness of an ill father and a harried mother who had little time for their only child.

"Stand up a minute," Emily held a wine-colored cotton throw in her hands. "You'll feel a lot more comfortable if you put this under you."

T.J. stood while Emily tossed the throw over the couch. Her bare arm brushed his bare arm, a curvaceous hip glanced his. He heard her gasp, noted her blush as she looked away.

T.J. was pleased. Emily might think she was through with him but that didn't seem to stop her from being aware of him or caring about him. Maybe that was a good sign. Easy does it, he told himself. He'd comment about the vintage furniture; furniture was definitely a safe subject. "If you stay, are you going to eventually change the furniture in here?"

"No." She glanced around the room. "Yes. Maybe," she amended as she wandered over to the piano. "But not right away, and certainly not the piano." She lifted the lid that covered the keyboard and idly fingered the keys. "Aunt Emily was a piano teacher. I used to fall asleep at night listening to her play. The sound of the metronome keeping time when she practiced scales used to lull me to sleep."

"Do you play, too," he asked softly, seeing Emily as a young girl.

"A little," she answered as she closed the keyboard's lid. "I was only interested in playing popular songs. As a piano teacher, my poor aunt was offended. My giving up piano was a mutual agreement."

T.J. sensed Emily was lost in recalling long-ago nights when piano music had eased her troubled young soul. He felt a surge of affection. Thank God for the Aunt Emily's of the world.

Visions of a young Emily impatiently practicing scales and sneaking in a popular tune intrigued him. "I never was any good at playing an instrument."

Emily eyed him thoughtfully. The time for friendly reminiscing was obviously over. "What was it you wanted to talk about?"

"Just this. Has it ever occurred to you that somehow our lives are entwined? That we have something in common and were destined to meet?"

She seemed to consider his question before she shook her head and sat down beside him on the couch. "I don't see how. I'd never met you until two weeks ago."

Emily dismissed him with a shrug, but the way she kept eyeing him told him she was just as aware of him as he was of her.

"I'm sorry you don't believe me." The last thing T.J. wanted was to antagonize the woman he'd fallen in love with. Not when he sensed he had her attention.

She had to believe him, their future depended on it. "I honestly believe the Kirkpatrick business of restoring old buildings had something to do with it. Fate had to have known I was the logical one to help you save the cottage."

"Now you're reaching for it," Emily answered, her mind obviously made up. "You've got it all wrong. It was your brother I actually met, remember? If he'd kept his word, I never would have looked you up. Besides, how could my aunt have known the Foundation for Homeless Children was going to sponsor a bachelor's auction? Or that I would show up in time to bid on your brother?"

"It does sound farfetched," T.J. agreed, "but I'm still convinced our meeting was supposed to happen. And furthermore," he added, putting his heart and soul into his voice, "I think there's actually some connection between us."

"Ridiculous," Emily dismissed him with a toss of her head. "I hadn't even thought of going to the auction until I saw the sign in the hotel lobby. I certainly never intended to spend $350 on a bachelor with the intent to have him pose as my husband. The idea came to me out of the blue."

"Aha!" T.J. felt vindicated. It was a sure sign Emily was as mystified over the circumstances of their unusual relationship as he was. "That's what I mean. *Something* made you to do it! Right?"

Emily gazed at him dubiously. It was true. Some voice, some impulse had prompted her to go inside the room where the auction was taking place. The same voice that had urged her to bid on Number 46.

She remembered the moment as clearly as if it had been yesterday. An embarrassed tingle ran through her when she remembered the way Number 46's sensuous gaze had affected her. And that her reaction had been tame compared to the way she'd physically reacted the first time she'd glimpsed all six feet of T.J. at the construction site.

"And how about the motion picture posters we saw in the hotel lobby? Another coincidence?"

Emily gazed into his winning smile. "Maybe," she finally said, "but not finding the movie posters behind the bedroom wall."

She stood up. "If that's all you came to tell me, you'd better leave."

Instead of leaving as she'd asked him to, T.J. looked as if he wanted to take her in his arms. Wary, she backed away before she found herself there.

He let loose his killer smile again. "I still think fate brought us together."

A shiver ran down Emily's spine. In some weird way, she found herself half believing him. The idea was frightening. "Please go now," she said before she made a fool of herself. "I have some packing to do."

"Wait a minute! You're not going home to Placerville, are you?"

"Yes, at least for a little while. But not before I get a copy of the title transfer and a copy of my aunt's will." She opened the screen door.

T.J. bit his lower lip as he forced himself to say goodbye. If he hadn't been able to convince Emily they belonged together, it was his fault. He had no concrete proof to back up his theory.

"EMILY HOLMES?"

Emily opened the door for the FedEx man. "Nice doorbell you have there," he commented approvingly. "Kinda reminds me of when I was a kid."

"Me, too," Emily replied. She signed for the package and remained in the doorway as the truck pulled away from the curb.

The package was from Daniels's secretary Maggie and obviously contained more than a will or a deed to the cottage. Maggie had come through for her, no doubt at T.J.'s urgings. She had a premonition that her life would never be the same once she opened it.

Holding the package to her breast, she wandered out onto the porch and sat down on the wooden swing. Swinging gently, she gazed over the canal to catch a glimpse of the ocean that glittered in the afternoon sun. Sailboats appeared on the horizon, their sails open to the brisk breeze. Seagulls glided lazily on the air current.

The peace and quiet of the moment, broken by a passing pedestrian was in sharp contrast to the excitement of the carnival. If it hadn't been for the newly built condos next door, the scene could have been the same one she remembered from her yearly visits to her aunt.

It was difficult to believe that it had been less than a month since she'd come to claim her inheritance, met T.J. and fallen in love with him. And only a few days since she'd sent him away after he'd broken her heart.

She stood, the FedEx package clutched unopened in her arms. Maybe it was just as well, she thought as she turned to go into the house. It was time, long past time, to put dreams aside and to get on with her life. First to go was the childhood dream of going to visit Italy. Her real life was here in Venice, California, with its canals outside her door.

The hardest to let go of was the dream of a loving husband and children she'd spun after she'd realized she'd fallen in love with T.J. And believed he'd loved her.

It wasn't only the subterfuge of letting her believe he was his brother that had awakened her to the real man. Nor his finding the vintage movie posters and not telling her, although heaven knows that was bad enough. Or that he hadn't realized right away she was a forever kind of woman.

It was his early hesitancy to commit to marriage because of the responsibilities he said he felt to his adoptive father. And his abrupt changes of heart that had made her feel she was on probation. They had kept them apart on and off and could someday come between them again.

She went to her aunt's bedroom and sat down in the oak rocking chair to open the package. A large envelope contained a cover note from Maggie, a copy of her aunt's will and a copy of the transferred deed. She read the note addressed to her.

Dear Miss Holmes,

After spending some time thinking about it, I decided you were entitled to the contents of a box your late aunt left with Mr. Daniels. Please don't tell anyone you have them until I have a chance to leave Los Angeles and go back to Montana where people are honest and tell the truth.

Sincerely,
Maggie Wilson

Emily frowned. What kind of documents were so private that her aunt hadn't wanted her to have them until now?

She opened the small, attached envelope and drew out a handwritten note.

Dearest Emily,

You were such a sweet, gentle, and vulnerable child whose life centered around make-believe that I hesitated to give these to you. I wanted you to remain untouched by reality until you were old enough to handle the realities of life on your own. Perhaps I was wrong. But I do want to tell you that you are, and always will be, not only my true grand-niece, but the child of my heart.

Lovingly,
Aunt Emily

Tears were sliding down her cheeks by the time Emily finished reading the note and drew out three official-looking documents.

First was a birth certificate, hers. "Father—unknown. Mother—Henrietta Bellows, Deceased. Cause of death—Childbirth."

A record of a health examination at her birth.

A certificate of her adoption when she was a few days old by a Vivian and Howard Holmes, her mother and father, was next.

Emily was thunderstruck. Her heart began to throb as though it would burst. Adopted? Her well-meaning mother and father were not her own? The aunt she'd loved more than any other person in the world and to whom she owed so much was not her real aunt?

She felt as if a roaring train had threatened to overtake her, to run over her. What was there left to believe in?

She sat there, slowly rocking away her initial re-action. The shock of realizing she'd been adopted slowly faded. She couldn't miss the real parents she'd never known. What had happened twenty-eight years ago had no effect on her life now. The only parents she'd ever known had loved her. Aunt Emily had loved and cherished her. What child could have asked for anything more?

She wiped the tears from her eyes, reached for her aunt's Bible, held it to her lips and whispered, "Thank you, Aunt Emily."

She may have lived in a world of make-believe when she was a child. Chosen a profession that sur-rounded her with other people's written dreams and dreamed her own. But now, at last, she felt ready for reality.

An inner strength surfaced as she thought of her protected childhood and secure future. Thanks to her aunt, she was financially able to follow any path she chose to follow. And, if T.J. was right, she had the right man to help her.

If she still wanted him.

A warm glow filled her as she finally began to

believe T.J. had been right about some connection between them. She began to understand why T.J. felt so grateful to his father for adopting him and his brother that that gratitude could have influenced the way he'd regarded marriage.

It was the same gratitude she felt for her aunt for all the loving years she'd given her. It was now up to her to convince T.J. once and for all that that kind of love didn't ask for repayment.

She glanced at her watch. Maybe it wasn't too late to tell T.J. so.

T.J. WAS STANDING at the door to the fire station talking to Tim when he heard hoots and hollers behind him. The kind of noises that red-blooded men make when they see a desirable woman. He tried to ignore them. He'd been down that road with disastrous results. One beautiful woman to break his heart was enough.

The whistles continued. "Hang on, Tim. I've got to go and cool down the jackasses out there. The way they're acting, you'd think they'd never seen a woman before."

"How do you know it's a dame?"

"I know. Believe me, I know."

"Wait for me," Tim answered, his blue eyes perking up. A broad smile curved at his lips. "Sounds as if it's going to be good."

"No thanks. Wait here," T.J. said, disgusted as

hell. "You've never met a woman you didn't like, and I have enough trouble on my hands already. Wait here. I'll be back as soon as I get rid of her."

He turned to go out and throw cold water on his crew, then froze. Golden rays of sunshine glinting in her auburn hair, Emily was coming up to meet him.

She wore her signature blue slip sundress and carried a small white box in her hand. He felt a strong sense of déjà vu, the past and the present became one.

"I had the hotel make you a box lunch," she said, echoing the words she'd first said to him two weeks ago. Dimples danced across her cheeks. The sensuous look in her eyes turned his knees to Jell-O.

T.J. swallowed hard. He was hungry all right, but it wasn't for the contents of the box lunch she carried. It was for the taste of her, the feel of her in his arms, the minty scent that had never left his thoughts.

Behind him, he heard Tim whistle.

"Get lost," T.J. said over his shoulder. The last thing he wanted was to have Tim anywhere near Emily. She belonged to him.

"Don't I even get a proper introduction?" Tim replied with a laugh as he came up behind T.J. "I was the guy that got the two of you together."

"No," T.J. replied, without taking his eyes off of

Emily's shining green eyes. "It was Emily's aunt
who accomplished the miracle. You were just the
means to put it into action."

"That's okay," Emily broke in, smiling at his
brother. "I'd like to thank you, Tim. After all,
you're going to be my brother-in-law."

T.J. dropped the blueprints he was carrying. This
was the moment he'd been waiting for. "He is?"

Emily nodded. A mischievous smile that pro-
ceeded to light up T.J.'s world covered her face.
"That is, if you still want me."

"I did, that is, I do." Having Emily at close quarters again was doing a number on him. All he could
think of was how to gracefully get her somewhere
private.

"First, we have to talk." She gazed around the
site and motioned to the lone tree. "Over there?"

"Sure," he answered, but his high spirits dropped
a notch. The fact that she was here was a good
omen. The fact that she still wanted to talk, wasn't.
He tossed the blueprints to Tim. "Let's go."

Emily made herself comfortable on the crate below the tree. Sunlight filtered through the tree
branches. "First, I have something to show you."
She took an official document out of the manila envelope she carried and handed it to him.

T.J. scanned it swiftly. "A birth certificate.
Yours?"

"Yes," she answered. "It came with this." She took another document out of the envelope. "I think this explains why we thought there was some connection between us."

T.J. studied the Certificate of Adoption issued by the Foundation for Homeless Children and signed by the Superior Court of California. Then he looked at her, the flush of color on her cheeks, the threat of tears in her eyes.

"That's mine, too," she said softly. "And furthermore, when I visited the foundation to ask about it, I saw my aunt's portrait in the lobby. She was not only on their board of directors at the time we both were born, she heavily endowed the foundation. Maybe, she was behind both adoptions."

T.J. dropped to the vacant crate beside her. "My God," he muttered. "That's the connection."

Emily nodded. "I called my mother, and she confirmed it. She also said she agreed with my aunt not to tell me about it until I was grown." She smiled ruefully. "She said they didn't have the heart to tell me because I was such a vulnerable little girl. I told her I wasn't a little girl anymore."

T.J. took her hands in his. "No, you're not. You're an intelligent, beautiful, caring woman. The woman I love. So, how about it. Will you marry me?"

"Yes." She went into his arms with a happy smile.

"Wow!" He grabbed Emily, lifted her arms and swung her around in the air to the accompanying sound of whistles. "Are you ready to get married? Tomorrow? Or better yet, today?"

Emily put her arms around his neck, inhaled his scent of sunshine and shaving lotion and laughed breathlessly. "Be careful, Tom," she said, clinging to him. "My feet can barely touch the ground!"

"They're never going to," he said, laughing up into her star-filled eyes. "Not as long as I have anything to say about it. From now on, Em, we're going to fly together. That is," he added as he captured her lips with his own, "if you're ready."

"I'm ready whenever you are," she whispered into his lips.

Two days later, they did.

Epilogue

"Em, sweetheart, wake up."

Emily groaned and burrowed deeper into her husband's arms. "Why?"

"Because today is our anniversary, that's why," he answered. He kissed the tip of her nose, nuzzled her in the sensitive spot behind her ear. "We've been married ten months today. You haven't forgotten, have you?"

Emily smiled drowsily and ran her hand over his cheek. Warm tingles of happiness ran through her. "You have to be the only man in the world to want to celebrate his wedding anniversary every month."

"Maybe so," he answered as he investigated a dimple on her cheek. "But it's fun reminding you."

"You don't have to remind me." She rubbed her hand across the gentle mound in her middle. "Emily Marie has a way of reminding me every day."

To Emily's delight, Tom slid down her flimsy

nightgown to put his cheek on her middle. "Hello, Emily Marie. This is your father speaking. I just wanted to tell you I can't wait to meet you."

Emily ran her fingers through Tom's hair and pressed him close to their unborn child, a child who was lucky to have him for a father.

"My two Emilys," Tom murmured. He slid back up to return her embrace. Cathedral chimes sounded outside the window. White doves cooed and fluttered against the horizon. "I hate to break this up, sweetheart, but the real Venice is waiting for us."

Emily looked out the curved window where cathedral spires appeared against a blue sky, where the voices of gondoliers drifted upward. As a child, she'd wished to come here, and now her husband had granted that wish.

"This is Venice, Italy," she said softly. "But you're right. The real Venice is back home."

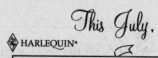

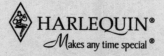

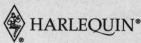

***USA Today* bestselling author**

STELLA CAMERON

and popular American Romance author

MURIEL JENSEN

come together in a special
Harlequin 2-in-1 collection.

Look for

Shadows and *Daddy in Demand*

On sale June 2001

HARLEQUIN®
Makes any time special®

Harlequin invites yo
to walk down the aisle..

To honor our year long celebration of weddin₁
we are offering an exciting opportunity for you
own the Harlequin Bride Doll. Handcrafted
fine bisque porcelain, the wedding doll is dress
for her wedding day in a cream satin gov
accented by lace trim. She carries an exquisi
traditional bridal bouquet and wears a cathedr₄
length dotted Swiss veil. Embroidered flowe
cascade down her lace overskirt to the scallop
hemline; underneath all is a multi-layered crinolin

Join us in our celebration of weddings by sending away for yc
own Harlequin Bride Doll. This doll regularly retails for $74.95 U.S./approx. $108.
CDN. One doll per household. Requests must be received no later than Decemb
31, 2001. Offer good while quantities of gifts last. Please allow 6-8 weeks for delive
Offer good in the U.S. and Canada only. Become part of this exciting offer!

Simply complete the order form and mail to:
"A Walk Down the Aisle"

IN U.S.A	IN CANADA
P.O. Box 9057	P.O. Box 622
3010 Walden Ave.	Fort Erie, Ontario
Buffalo, NY 14269-9057	L2A 5X3

Enclosed are eight (8) proofs of purchase found in the last pages
every specially marked Harlequin series book and $3.75 check
money order (for postage and handling). Please send my Harlequ
Bride Doll to:

Name (PLEASE PRINT)

Address   Apt. #

City   State/Prov.   Zip/Postal Code

Account # (if applicable)   **097 KIK DAEᴠ**

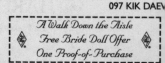

HARLEQUIN®
Makes any time special ®

Visit us at www.eHarlequin.com

```
┌─────────────────────────────────┐
│  A Walk Down the Aisle          │
│  Free Bride Doll Offer          │
│  One Proof-of-Purchase          │
└─────────────────────────────────┘
```

PHWDAPOPR2